I0634860

Hall Caine

The Scapegoat

A Romance. Vol. 1

Hall Caine

The Scapegoat
A Romance. Vol. 1

ISBN/EAN: 9783337020897

Printed in Europe, USA, Canada, Australia, Japan

Cover: Foto ©Andreas Hilbeck / pixelio.de

More available books at **www.hansebooks.com**

THE SCAPEGOAT

A ROMANCE

E SCAPEGOAT

A ROMANCE

By HALL CAINE

AUTHOR OF

"*THE BONDMAN,*" *AND* "*THE DEEMSTER*"

"*Thy will be done on earth*"

IN TWO VOLUMES

VOL. I.

LONDON

WILLIAM HEINEMANN

1891

NOTE

My thanks are due to Chief Rabbi Adler, for opening to my observation the homes and lives of the Sephardic Jews of Morocco; to Mr. Israel Abraham, Editor of the Jewish Quarterly Review, *and to another Jewish scholar, for guidance in Jewish ceremonial law; to the Sub-Editor of the* Lancet *for the opinion of medical experts; and to Mr. Ion Perdicaris of Tangier, and Mr. J. E. Budgett Meakin, late Editor of the* Times of Morocco, *for important help in nearly all that concerns the local atmosphere of my story. Also I am once more indebted to my fellow-countryman, the author of " Fo'c's'le Yarns," for spontaneous and unacknowledged collaboration at various points. But, not to make my friends responsible either for my errors or my fancies, I must needs confess that, though I have spared no pains to be true to plain fact and possibility, my heart has been so much occupied with the spiritual love of a noble man and a beautiful woman, that my book is less novel than romance, and less romance than poem.*

CONTENTS

THE SCAPEGOAT

INTRODUCTION.

Within sight of an *English port*, and within hail of *English ships as they pass on to our empire in the East, there is a land where the ways of life are the same to day as they were a thousand years ago : a land wherein government is oppression, wherein law is tyranny, wherein justice is bought and sold, wherein it is a terror to be rich and a danger to be poor, wherein man may still be the slave of man, and woman is no more than a creature of lust—a reproach to Europe, a disgrace to the century, an outrage on humanity, a blight on religion ! That land is Morocco !*

This is a story of Morocco in the last years of the Sultan Abd er-Rahman. The ashes of that tyrant are cold, and his grandson sits in his place; but men who earned his displeasure linger yet in his noisome dungeons, and women who won his embraces are starving at this hour in the prison-palaces in which he immured them. His reign is a story of yesterday; he is gone, he is forgotten; no man so meek and none so mean but he might spit upon his tomb. Yet the evil work which he did in his evil time is done to-day, if not by his grandson, then in his grandson's name—the degradation of man's honour, the cruel wrong of woman's, the shame of base usury, and the iniquity of justice that may be bought! Of such corruption this story will tell, for it is a tale of tyranny that is every day repeated, a voice of suffering going up hourly to the powers of the world, calling on them to forget the secret hopes and petty jealousies whereof Morocco is a cause, to think no more of any scramble for territory when the fated day of that doomed land has come, and only to look to it and see that he who fills the throne of Abd er-Rahman shall be the last to sit there.

AFTER a weary journey in the central provinces, coming up from Fez by way of Wazzán, I chanced to arrive at Tetuan at a time of great excitement. It was the eve of the chief feast of the Mohammedan year, the feast of the birthday of the Prophet. That of itself must have been a cause of sufficient commotion, for the sect of the Âïssáwà were expected from Mequinez, and every one knew that before the seven days of the feast had ended the streets of the town must flow with the blood of the wildest of the fanatics of Islam. But it was an event of still deeper solemnity and yet grander magnificence that set in motion the poor people of Tetuan. His Shereefian Majesty, their Sultan Abd er-Rahman, had announced an intention of keeping the feast in their midst.

Throughout the preceding month the Sultan had been among the Reef mountains with his motley army of foot and horse, making one of his accustomed raids on a rebellious tribe of his people, for the enforcement of the tribute they had refused to pay. Once again his arms had conquered, he had driven the mountaineers back into their fastnesses, confiscated all they had abandoned, devastated their homes, and left their villages in flames behind him. Thus having finished the work which he had set his hand to do, he bethought him of the feast of the birthday of Mohammed, and so it befell that, being nearest to Tetuan of the greater towns of his empire, he had concluded that he would say his prayers there, the better that he might meanwhile quarter his big army on the town's inhabitants.

On the evening of my arrival the Sultan had been heard of about four hours away, encamped with his Ministers, a portion of his hareem, and a detachment of his army, somewhere by the foot of Beni Hosmar. His entry was fixed for eight o'clock next morning, and preparations for his coming were everywhere afoot. Not in loyalty and certainly not in love did the townsfolk busy themselves for the reception of their prince, but nevertheless all other occupations were at a standstill, and nothing was to be heard but the noise and clamour of the cleansing of the streets, and the hanging of flags and of carpets. Only with difficulty, after much importunity and

many protests, had I prevailed upon the deputy of
the Governor to assign me a lodging for the night.
When at length I had secured it, and had moved
into it with my guide and companion, Jellali, I found
it a damp, dark, and dirty little den under the
shadow of the western gate. It was the first place
for a casual stranger which had come to the Khaleefa's
knowledge, and it had been thrust upon me because
it gave least trouble.

Protest, I well knew, would be vain, and, as much
in pity of the confusion of the officials, as in disgust
at my surroundings, I had made up half a mind to
relieve both of my presence, and, late as it was, set
out from the town again, in the hope of reaching
before night the fondak that lies in the plains between
Tetuan and Tangier.

I was the more inclined to this course from un-
willingness to witness the spectacle of the morning.
What the townspeople looked to with interest, if not
enthusiasm, I regarded in advance with languor, if
not distaste. Loyalty I had none, and love I had

less than none, for the tyrant that was to come on the morrow. The Sultan was nothing to me but a heartless sensualist with a black face, and not even the barbaric splendour of his train had a moment's power to hold me. I had seen both already, first at Mequinez and again at Fez; I was travelling under the name and mockery of the Sultan's protection. I had spoken with his dusky Majesty; his evil eyes had smiled upon me, and the loaded fingers of his clumsy hand had touched for me his dazzling breast. Hence I found little interest and no novelty, but certain discomfort and probable danger, in the freedom of such a day of license as the Sultan's visit to Tetuan would surely be to me.

That I did not leave the town the same night, having so strong an impulse to go, was partly due to a passive protest from my man Jellali. The poor fellow was worn out with fatigue. I was myself no less weary. We had travelled far that day; the sun had been hot, our mules had been stubborn, and the tracks that serve as roads had been deep and ugly.

"Jellali," I said, after another glance at the reeking walls of our lodgings, "spread the mattresses on the roof: we shall sleep there to-night."

"Blessings on your beard!" cried Jellali—at that time a superfluous prayer.

I could laugh to think of it, now that by so paltry a chance the central fact of my life was brought about. Yet, why should I laugh at chance? Is it not the master of human destiny? The great thing that we did of set design and purpose, where is it when the whole reckoning of our life is made? But the little thing that chance did for us, is it not the pivot whereon our fate has turned? And surely nothing but the Book of Fate itself had willed it that, coming by chance, and remaining against my inclination, I was in Tetuan on the day of the entry of the Sultan Abd er-Rahman. Can I doubt it as I raise my eyes and look about me where I write? It is evening, in a quiet room of an English house looking out on an English garden, where the hawthorn and the lilac bloom together, and the blackbird sings unseen from

the beech-tree by the wall. Jellali himself is here, as
sly as of old, and as faithful too, somewhat aged since
his transplantation, and visibly somewhat happier.
But it is not Jellali's tawny face and crimson kaftan
only that tells in my English home of the distant
land of the prickly pear and the long aloe. *She* is
here; she is by my side—she whom my eyes had not
seen—strange as it is to think that she can ever have
been absent from my sight—until the early sunlight
of that day in Tetuan brought the best of all sunlight
into my life.

It was a wonderful night. The air was cool, for
the year was deep towards winter, but not a breath
of wind was stirring, and the orange gardens behind
the town wall did not send over the river so much as
the whisper of a leaf. Stars were out, and the big
moon of the East shone white on the white walls and
minarets. It was late when I went up to my mat-
tress on the flat roof of our unwholesome dwelling, and
then the traffic of the streets was done and the town
was quiet. Nowhere is night so full of the spirit of

sleep as in an Eastern city. Below, under the moonlight, lay the square white roofs, and between them
were the dark streets going in and out, trailing
through and along, like to narrow streams of black
water in a bed of quarried chalk. Here or there,
where a belated townsman lit himself homeward with
a lamp, a red light gleamed out of one of the thin
darknesses, crept along a few paces, and then was
gone. Sometimes a clamour of voices came up with
their own echo from some unseen place, and again
everything was still. Sleep, sleep, all was sleep. I
gathered my cloak and rugs about me, and lay down
for the night.

In the first grey of morning I was awakened by
the chant of the mooddin from a minaret near at
hand—

"Sleep is good, but prayer is better. God is
great! God is great!"

I had heard it before, and had passed the stage of
Eastern experience when to the unbelieving ear that
wail over a sleeping town is pleasant. So I groaned

and shuddered, gathered my garments yet closer together, and tried to sleep again.

But there was to be no more rest that night. I was hardly conscious that I had slept, before a street-crier came, beating a drum, and crying in a hoarse voice, "Awake! Awake! Come and greet your Lord! Awake! Awake!"

What the sumner of the Lord of Hosts had not done, the sumner of the Lord Sultan very speedily brought to pass. In a little while the streets were alive with motley and noisy crowds. A vague and confused perception of this came to me at first through the outposts of slumber; but soon the cries of some of the people, and the laughter of others, fell in upon me where I lay, and, early as it was, I arose.

And being risen, though in moody temper, I could not but allow to myself that it was a gorgeous sight I looked upon. The sun was up, if still red and hazy, and the sunlight came like a tunnel of gold down the swampy valley and from over the sea.

Some orange orchards lying to the south, called the gardens of the Sultan, were red rather than yellow, and the snowy crests of the mountain heights above them were crimson rather than white. In the town itself the small red flag that is the Moorish ensign seemed to hang out from every house, and carpets of many colours swung on many walls. Certainly Tetuan was a wondrous sight already.

The sun was not yet high before the Sultan's army began to arrive. It was a mixed and noisy throng that came first, a sort of ragged regiment of Arabs, with long guns, and with their gun-cases wrapped about their heads—a big gang of wild country-folk lately enlisted as soldiers. They poured into the town at the western gate, and shuffled and jostled and squeezed their way through the narrow streets, firing recklessly into the air, and shouting as they went, " Abd er-Rahman is coming! The Sultan is coming! Dogs! Men! Believers! Infidels! Come out! come out!"

Thus they went puffing along, covered with dust

and sweltering in perspiration, and at every fresh shot and shout the streets they passed through grew denser. But it was a grim satire on their lawless loyalty that almost at their heels there came into the town, not the Sultan himself, but a troop of his prisoners from the mountains. Ten of them there were in all, guarded by ten soldiers, and they made a sorry spectacle. They were chained together, man to man in single file, not hand to hand or leg to leg, but neck to neck. So had they walked a hundred miles, never separated night or day, either sleeping or waking, or faint or strong. The feet of some were bare and torn, and dripping blood. The faces of all were black with grime, and streaked with lines of sweat. And thus they toiled into the streets in that sunlight of God's own morning, under the red ensigns of Morocco, by the many-coloured carpets of Rabat, to the Kasbah beyond the market-place. They were Reefians whose homes the Sultan had just stripped, whose villages he had just burnt, whose wives and children he had just driven into the mountains. And they were going to die in his dungeons.

It was seven o'clock by this time, and rumour had it that the Sultan's train was moving down the valley. From the roof of my lodging by the gate I could see something swarming across the plain in the distance. Then came some rapid transformations of the scene below. First the streets were deserted by every decent blue jellab and clean white turban within range of sight. These presently reappeared on the roofs of the principal thoroughfare, where groups of women, closely covered in their haiks, had already begun to congregate with their dark attendants. Next, a body of the townsmen who possessed firearms mounted guard on the walls to protect the town from the lawlessness of the big army that was coming. Then into the Feddán, the square market-place, came pouring from their own little quarter within its separate walls a throng of Jewish people, in their black kaftans and skull-caps, men and women and children, carrying banners that bore loyal inscriptions, twanging at tambourines and crying in wild discords, " God bless our Lord ! " " God give victory to our Lord the Sultan ! "

The poor Jews got small thanks for such loyalty to the last of the Caliphs of the Prophet. Every ragged Moor in the streets greeted them with exclamations of menace and abhorrence. Even the blind beggar crouching at the gate lifted up his voice and cursed them.

" Get out, you Jew ! God burn your father ! Dogs, take off your slippers—Abd er-Rahman is coming ! "

Thus they were scolded and abused on every side, kicked, cuffed, jostled, and wedged together well-nigh to suffocation. Their banners were torn out of their hands, their tambourines were broken, their voices were drowned, and finally they were driven back into their Mellah and shut up there, and forbidden to look upon the entry of the Sultan, even from their roofs.

And the vagabonds and ragamuffins among the faithful in the streets, having got rid of the unbelievers, had enough ado to keep peace among themselves. They pushed and struggled and stormed and cried and laughed and clamoured down this main artery of the town through which the Sultan's train must pass. Men and boys, women also and young girls, donkeys with packs, bony mules too, and at least one dirty and terrified old camel. It was a confused and uproarious Babel. Angry black faces thrust into white ones, flashing eyes and gleaming white teeth, and clenched fists uplifted. Human voices barking like dogs, yelping like hyenas, shrill and guttural, piercing and grating. Prayings, beggings, quarrellings, cursings.

" Arrah! Arrah! Arrah!"

" O Merciful! O Giver of good to all!"

" Curses on your grandfather!"

" Allah! Allah! Allah!"

" Bálak! Bálak! Bálak!"

But presently the wild throng fell into order and silence. The gate of the Kasbah was thrown open, and a line of soldiers came out, headed by the Kaid

of Tetuan, the Governor of the town, and moved on
towards the city wall. The rabble were thrust back,
the soldiers were drawn up in lines on either side
of the street, and the Kaid himself took a position
by the western gate.

This man was then almost facing me, where I
stood with my servant on the roof of my lodging,
yet so much were my eyes and ears engaged by the
sights and sounds of the streets that I should not
have seen or heard him, nor should I to this day
have any distinct impression of what manner of man
he was to look upon—great as the part has been that
his conduct has played in my life—but that he himself drew my attention upon him. It was now eight
o'clock, the sun was high, and I had put up an umbrella to protect my head from the heat. No
thought had I given to my poor little alpaca in
relation to the proceedings of the day that it was
any dishonour to the Shereefian majesty, who alone
in his own presence must be so sheltered, nor had
any one in the streets or on the roofs appeared to

notice it, but the eye of the Kaid caught it instantly from his seat on his charger that was prancing under the arch. It would seem that he called on me to close it; but I did not hear him, and neither was Jellali conscious of his command. Then without more ado he ordered a guard by his side to fire upon it, and I first became aware of my own offence, and of the Governor's presence, in having my luckless umbrella riddled in my hand by a dexterous shot from a long-barrelled flint-lock.

At that I closed it promptly, and proceeded to take note of the Kaid. He was an elderly man, riding a chestnut horse, having gorgeous trappings of crimson cloth and gold. His dress was hardly less brilliant—a chocolate jellab over a kaftan of several colours. There was negro blood in him, for his complexion was of the deepest brown, and his nostrils and lips were wide and heavy. His eyes were hazel, and the white of them was streaked and bleared. Under his turban the short curls of his hair were iron grey. It was an evil face, selfish, heartless, and cruel.

By this time there was a commotion on the town walls among the townsmen who had taken up positions there. The Sultan's army was drawing near, a confused and disorderly mass of human beings moving on from the plain. As they came up to the walls, we who were standing on the house roofs could see them, and as they were ordered away to encamp by the river, none could help but hear their shouts and oaths.

When the motley and noisy concourse had been driven off to their camping ground, the gates of the town were thrown wide, for the Sultan himself was at hand. This, which was the crisis of interest to the townsfolk, bringing to their feet those who had been squatting on the housetops, was to me a moment of little consequence. Hitherto I had been absorbed in sights such as an Eastern town only on its gala day can show. With the coming of the Sultan's train my interest seemed to end, and, by that strange perversity of fate which coquets with us sometimes at our highest moments, I had half an

impulse to turn away before the red umbrella of
royalty had come in sight, or I had first beheld that
face which of all faces has since been the light of
my life. Nevertheless, by another whim of fate's
coquetry, I remained where I was standing, looking
languidly down on a spectacle that I had seen before,
and had little desire to see again.

There, as at the capital, came the two soldiers afoot,
and then followed the five artillery men with their
small pieces packed on mules. There, too, came the
mounted standard-bearers four deep, some in red,
some in blue, and some in green. There, again,
came the outrunners and the spearmen, and then the
Sultan's six led horses. It was all as I had seen it
at Fez. And there at length, with the great umbrella held over him, came the Sultan himself, the
elderly sensualist, with his dusky cheeks, his rheumy
eyes, his thick lips, and his heavy nostrils. The
fat Father of Islam was mounted that day on a
snow-white stallion, bedecked in gorgeous trappings.
Its bridle was of green silk, embroidered in gold.

Solomon's seal was stamped on its head-gear, and
the tooth of a boar—a safeguard against the evil eye
—was suspended from its neck. Its saddle was of
orange damask, with girths of stout silk, and its
stirrups were of chased silver. The Sultan's own
trappings were of the colour of his horse. His
kaftan was of white cloth, with an embroidered
leathern girdle ; his turban was of white cotton,
and his kisá was also white and transparent.

As he passed under the archway of the town's
gate the cannon of the Kasbah boomed forth a salute,
the Kaid dismounted and kissed his stirrup, and the
crowds in the streets burst upon him with blessings.

"God bless our Lord !"

" Sultan Abd er-Rahman ! "

" God prolong the life of our Lord ! "

He seemed hardly to hear them. Once his hand
touched his breast when the Kaid approached
him. After that he looked neither to the right
nor to the left, nor gave any sign of pleasure or
recognition. Nevertheless the people in the streets

ceased not to greet him with deafening acclama-
tions.

" All's well, all's well," they told each other, and
pointed to the white horse—the sign of peace—
which the Sultan rode, and to the riderless black
horse—the sign of strife—that pranced behind
him.

The women on the housetops also, in their hooded
cloaks, welcomed the Sultan with a shrill ululation :
" Yoo-yoo, yoo-yoo, yoo-yoo ! "

Not content with this, the usual greeting of their
sex and nation, some of them who had hitherto been
closely veiled threw back their muslin coverings,
exposed their faces to his face, and welcomed him
with more articulate cries.

He gave them neither a smile nor a glance, but
rode straight onward. Beside him walked the fly-
flappers, flapping the air before his podgy cheeks
with long scarfs of silk, and behind him rode his
Ministers of State, five sleek dogs who daily fed his
appetites on carrion that his head might be like

his stomach, and their power over him thereby the greater.

My gorge rose at the spectacle. This tyrant had done nothing for his people but take their taxes. Not a man had he protected from injustice; not a woman had he saved from dishonour. Never a rich usurer among them but trembled at his messages, nor a poor wretch but dreaded his dungeons. His law existed only for himself; his government had no object but to collect his dues. And yet there he was, going down the street amid wild vociferations of welcome.

Fear, fear! Fear it was in the heart of the rich man on the housetop, whose moneys were hidden, as well as in the darkened soul of the blind beggar at the gate whose eyes had been gouged out long ago because he dared not divulge the secret place of his wealth.

I turned my own eyes away. And then, while all other eyes, above and below, on the roofs, on the walls, and on the pavement, followed the Sultan down the street, I saw—I alone, save my man Jellali—a scene enacted, a trifling scene, a momentary incident, which I regard as the central fact of my own life, and at least the beginning of this story.

After the Ministers of State came a part of the royal hareem. This feature of the procession was new to me, and I looked upon it with freshened interest. The ladies, all but one of their number, rode on mules and were attended by eunuchs. She who did not so ride sat in a crimson litter swung between two small milk-white Arab horses, with trappings of pale-green silk. Midway she came in a line of about twelve, and, like the others, she was closely veiled and jealously watched.

Now this, I thought, having regard for the special gaiety of her surroundings, must be the latest favourite of her master and husband, happy in her new splendour, envied by her rival sisters, revelling for a while in their jealous anger, and recking not at all of the time that will come so soon when she too, like them, must give place to yet another concubine.

" God pity the poor little fool ! " I said to myself,
and even while the words were on my lips a strange
thing happened.

The first of the horses that bore the litter stumbled
into a hole in the unpaved way at the moment when
it was abreast of me. I thought the lurch must
throw the rider into the street, and she seemed to
fear the same disaster, for she flung out both her
hands to break the fall. At the next instant the
horse had recovered his feet, the watchful eunuch in
attendance had restored the scattered veils, and the
crimson litter was moving away. But in that quick
instant I had seen the face of her who sat in it.

What shall I say of that face ? By later knowledge and calmer observation I could tell of the colour
of the eyes and of the mould of the features. But
what would so poor an inventory avail to make that
face live before you now as it then lived before me ?
Of the colour of those eyes I was unconscious, and of
the mould of those features I knew nothing. Not for
my life could I have told you then whether the face

was dark or fair. Only one thing came to me, only
a single impression—an impression of startling un-
likeness of what I had thought of and expected.
Only this, during that swift moment of first sight,
and then, when it was over, and the face that I had
seen as by lightning was again covered and had
gone, a sense of sudden gloom, as if the sun had been
blotted out.

But at the next instant, with recovered consciousness, I realised in part by the mirror of the mind's
eye the features that had possessed me. The face
was not swarthy, but pale to pallidness. Neither
was it Moorish nor Arab nor Berber nor Negro in its
cast, but of that type—as I thought—that is loveliest
among the creatures of God—the type of a beautiful
English girl. And, above all else, the eyes where I
had looked for pride and vanity, and the light of
triumph, were big and soft and liquid, and seemed to
be on the point of breaking into tears. Sadness,
pain, and even anguish made up the expression of
that startling face. And, framed by such surround-

ings, the impression it made upon me was over-powering.

By a quick rebound my mind went back to the bestial half-black sensualist who had just gone past me under the red umbrella, and I turned away from the procession and saw no more of it. What happened next I hardly knew, save that the town gates had been closed to shut out the rabble of the Sultan's army, and that I was seated in the little patio of my lodging before the breakfast that Jellali had prepared for me. But I could not eat; the coffee had no flavour, the dates no juice; I was sickening with a sense of I knew not yet what horror. Now I know well what horror it was: it was the horror of that girl in that procession.

Who was she? What was she? It was folly to ask. Her belongings seemed to bespeak her class and condition. She was a wife of the Sultan Abd er-Rahman. Or, since his faith forbade that he should have more than four wives, she was probably his concubine. And yet that white face, those

English features, and the great soft eyes! Strange
and incongruous spectacle! What mystery lay
hidden in it? What sadness? What tragedy?

I resolved that Jellali should read me the riddle.
He was a Moor and a Mohammedan, and could ask
questions without exciting suspicions. But when I
proposed the task to him he was thrown into con-
vulsions of dread. I have said that he alone, besides
myself, seemed to have seen the girl's face. He did
not deny that he had seen it, and therein lay his
terror. It was death to a subject of the Sultan to
have beheld the face of the Sultan's wife, and Jellali
was full of stories of the penalty of such a transgression. I saw no reason to fear, for it was one
thing to have seen the face of a Sultan's wife, and
another thing to be known to have seen it. In any
case, my irrational determination was fixed. At all
risks, Jellali should go to the servants of the Governor,
with whom he had foregathered already, while
arrangements for our lodging were pending, and
find out who and what and whence was the lady

who rode in the crimson litter swung between milk-white ponies.

While he was gone I went out to the market-place, being too restless to remain indoors, though the heat was now great; and there, before a multitude of excited spectators, certain tribes of mountaineers were going through their feats of powder-play. A month before I had seen it all at Mequinez, and had thought it then a thrilling and splendid exhibition; but here it seemed merely frantic and barbaric. Two tribes, mounted on wild barbs, charged in line from opposite sides of the square—some seated, some kneeling, some standing. Midway across the market-place they changed horses at full gallop, fired their muskets, then reined in at a horse's length, threw their barbs on their haunches, wheeled round and galloped back, amid deafening shouts of " Allah!" " Allah !" " Allah !" Yes, yes, that was all the part that God played in this land where woman was no better than a slave.

When I returned home Jellali was waiting for me

with startling intelligence. The lady of the crimson litter was not a wife of Abd er-Rahman, and neither was she yet his concubine. She was a present that the Governor had that very morning sent out as a peace-offering to the Sultan on his entry into the town !

I was bewildered. To be given as a present the girl must surely be a slave. But what slave-girls were there now except Negresses from beyond the Atlas? Was white slavery not yet extinct in Morocco ? And then the girl's English face ! What devil's work could be afoot ?

By this time my head was hot and my heart aflame. I remembered a hundred bitter stories of earlier English captives, and already I saw myself galloping to the English Minister at Tangier with a wild tale of outraged honour. But Jellali must go back to the servants of the Governor and learn more. Who was the girl that the Kaid of Tetuan had that day presented to the Sultan ?

To beguile the time of Jellali's absence, and cheat

my nerves of my impatience, I went away through the little postern gate of the town to where the great body of the Sultan's army lay encamped by the river under the walls. The townsfolk who had shut the soldiers out, with all the rabble of their following, had nevertheless sent them fifty camels' load of kesksoo, the common dish of the country, and it was being served in equal parts, half a pound to each man. Where this meal had already been eaten, the usual charlatans of the market-place were busily plying their accustomed trades. Black jugglers from Soos, sham snake-charmers from the desert, and story-tellers both grave and facetious, all twanging their hideous ginbri—the two-stringed Moorish instrument—were seated on the ground in half-circles of soldiers and their women. Such amusements were of a piece with everything else. To be deceived, and know you were being deceived, was a fit pleasure in a land wherein all life was a deception.

My heart fell low at the news which Jellali brought back with him. The girl was not an English captive

—I had been mad to think she might be—but the daughter of a Moorish Jew, a subject of the Sultan. The father's name was Israel ben Oliel. He had lived nearly thirty years in the town, and his house could be seen in the Mellah. During a large part of that time he had been a man of great power in Tetuan, standing high in the favour of the Kaid, and being master of all other men of whatsoever class and condition, civil and military, Moor and Jew. And the girl—her name was Naomi. She had fallen into the Kaid's hands on some accusation relating to her faith. A month ago she had been cast into prison at the Kasbah, and since then she had been condemned to death. Only this morning, either at her own concession or at the Kaid's caprice, she had been liberated in order that she might be offered as a present to the Sultan.

What could I do? The girl was a subject of Abd er-Rahman, and Abd er-Rahman would surely have his will of her. Not all the casual strangers in Morocco dare lift a finger on her behalf. Nevertheless, I would find her father, and he should tell me her offence.

I knew it must be an idle errand, but I made my way to the Mellah. The "place of the salt" stands in its separate walls on the south-east of the market-place, and near the south-east corner of the Mellah itself stands the house of the father of Naomi. I found it the largest and finest building in the quarter, half Moorish with its open patio, half European with its windows and doors. But it was empty; it was a wreck, and in its battered and shattered condition it looked as if the fury of some mob had destroyed it. What did all this mean?

Two middle-aged Jews, with hands in their upright pockets, stood leaning against a neighbouring wall. I recognised them as of the number of those who had been hustled and cuffed in the morning. Could they tell me anything of Israel ben Oliel? No. Was he dead? No. Was he in prison? Not now. Then what had befallen him? Who could tell? What had been the charge against his daughter? God alone could say.

It was useless to ask. Fear, fear! The accursed monster, with watchful eyes on every side of it, was the quivering thing whereon the whole mockery of government rested. And Naomi! I would take the word of that unhappy face for as much as my life was worth. This morning in the hideous prison of the Kasbah, and doomed to-night to the more hideous arms of that black voluptuary. There was villainy somewhere, if a man could but find it out.

Returning to my lodging, I found the streets cleared for the mad antics of the Aïssáwà. When darkness fell they came forth, a score of half-naked men, and one other entirely naked, attended by their high-priests, the Mukaddameen, three old patriarchs with long white beards, wearing dark flowing robes and carrying torches. Then goats and sheep and dogs and cats were riven alive and eaten raw; while women and children, crouching in the darkness over-head, looked down from the roofs and shuddered. And as the frenzy increased among the madmen, and their victims became fewer, each fanatic turned upon himself, and tore his own skin and battered his head against the stones, until blood ran like water, and the street was a sickening sewer.

I turned from the sight with loathing. What offence against religion could have been made by that soft-eyed girl of the morning, if these barbarians of the night were hereby doing it honour?

When I reached home I found Jellali waiting with yet another piece of news for me. The lady of the crimson litter had suddenly fallen sick and insensible, and had been taken back from the palace to the Kasbah. Cruel as it may seem to say it, my heart leapt up to hear that Naomi was ill and in prison.

Yet why should I rejoice at whatever less terrible fate befell this girl to whom I was a stranger, this girl who was a stranger to me? She was a victim of some base injustice—true. She was unhappy—also true. But in a land where woman was a chattel, and beauty a thing for sale and barter, she had not been the first, and would not be the last, in that same condition. And, above all and before all, whatever her wrongs, I was powerless to relieve them.

I resolved to leave Tetuan the following day. Not all the terrors of all the Jinoon of Islam should keep me there after the earliest light of morning.

The mooddin was chanting the call to prayers, and the old porter at the gate was muttering over his rosary as we left the town in the dawn. We had to pick our way among the soldiers who were lying on the bare soil outside, uncovered to the sky. Not one of them seemed to be awake. Even their camels were still sleeping, nose to nose in the circles where they had last fed. Only their mules and asses, all hobbled and still saddled, were up and feeding.

Though so late in the year, the morning was soft and beautiful, and I whistled as I rode, and told myself what joy it was merely to be alive. When this diversion failed me I took to noting the foliage and the fruit, the prickly pear and the long-leaved aloe, the myrtle and the twisted cactus, the quince trees and the figs. Such things served me with an effort, between various loud squabbles with my mule, while we were crossing the low-lying plain beyond the bridge from which Tetuan may not be seen. But when we had risen out of it to that point abreast of the village of Semsa, from which the town is said to look like Jerusalem. I could not help but pause, that I might take one first and last look backward.

Yonder it lay in the sunlight, with the snow-tipped heights above it and the broad sea at its back, the place we had just left, a white thing surrounded by orange orchards. And, gazing back at it from there, I knew then for the first time my own new-born secret. What I was leaving behind me was not Tetuan only, but a sudden and hopeless and irrational love. No matter; my short dream was over; I was awake at last.

How whimsical is that coquetry of fate! Less than half an hour afterwards I stumbled upon a fact which altered all my views of life. Riding at the mule's walking pace, with a mind full of recollections of the spectacle of yesterday, thinking with bitterness of its

barbaric splendour, and with sadness of the sorrowful
face so strangely placed in it, coming near to the
fondak, where travellers rest on their journeys, I lit
on the wreck of a hut, and an old man sitting at the
door of it.

So poor a place, I thought, I had not seen in all
my wanderings through that abject land. Its walls
were of clay that was bulged and cracked, and its
roof was of rushes which lay over it like sea-wrack
on a broken barrel. The old man was clearly a Jew;
his clothing was one worn and torn kaftan; his feet
were shoeless and his head was bare. Poverty and
misery sat on him, and squalor was about his home.
But his face arrested me. It was a big, strong face,
with a snow-white beard. His hair, too, was long
and white. A Jovian head, and a countenance with
some of the grander lines of the ancient and heroic
race of Israel—how did they come to be here and
in a case like this?

I drew up beside the old man as he sat in his doorway. He did not appear to see me. And then,

being nearer to him, I noticed that his big grey eyes had a look of madness. He was talking with himself, and I could not help but hear. Neither could I help but listen, for he was speaking in the English tongue. He was mumbling terms of endearment, coupled sometimes with a name. And what name was it? I thought my ears deceived me: I thought my heart must be ringing an echo of one only name through my troubled head. But, no; the name the old man muttered in his madness, with words of love around it, was no other than Naomi.

Naomi! Could this be the father of her whom I had seen amid the dazzling splendour of the Sultan's procession? I hastened to the fondak and asked, and found my conclusions to be right. This, then, was Israel ben Oliel; this was the man who for near thirty years had stood high in the favour of the Kaid of Tetuan, being master there of all other men whomsoever: this was the father of Naomi; and while she lay ill and in prison, and in imminent peril of a more terrible fate, he was here in this unhappy plight—deaf, nearly blind, and insane at intervals.

My curiosity, as well as my pity and my affection, had by this time been engaged. If I could do nothing to relieve the wrongs of these people, I could at least satisfy my interest in the facts of their history.

"Jellali," I cried, wheeling my mule about, "we are going back to Tetuan."

We went back straightway, and there we stayed during the remaining days of the feast of the Moolood. But before the feast had ended I had learned all I know of the strange story of Israel and Naomi. I shall relate its facts in their rightful order, not intruding again on my narrative until I come to tell of those closing incidents wherein I too played a part.

CHAPTER I.

ISRAEL was the son of a Jewish banker at Tangier. His mother was the daughter of a banker in London. The father's name was Oliel; the mother's was Sara. Oliel had held business connections with the house of Sara's father, and he came over to England that he might have a personal meeting with his correspondent. The English banker lived over his office, near Holborn Bars, and Oliel met with his family. It consisted of one daughter by a first wife, long dead, and three sons by a second wife, still living. They were not altogether a happy household, and the chief apparent cause of discord was the child of the first wife in the home of the second. Oliel was a man of quick perception, and he saw the difficulty. That was how it came about that he was married to Sara.

When he returned to Morocco he was some thousand pounds richer than when he left it, and he had a capable and personable wife into his bargain.

Oliel was a self-centred and silent man, absorbed in getting and spending, always taking care to have much of the one, and no more than he could help of the other. Sara was a nervous and sensitive little woman, hungering for communion and for sympathy. She got little of either from her husband, and grew to be as silent as himself. With the people of the country of her adoption, whether Jews or Moors, she made no headway. She never even learnt their language.

Two years passed, and then a child was born to her. This was Israel, and for many a year thereafter he was all the world to the lonely woman. His coming made no apparent difference to his father. He grew to be a tall and comely boy, quick and bright, and inclined to be of a sweet and cheerful disposition. But the school of his upbringing was a hard one. A Jewish child in Morocco might know from his cradle that he was not born a Moor and a Mohammedan.

When the boy was eight years old his father married a second wife, his first wife being still alive. This was lawful, though unusual in Tangier. The new marriage, which was only another business transaction to Oliel, was a shock and a terror to Sara. Nevertheless, she supported its penalties through three weary years, sinking visibly under them day after day. By that time a second family had begun to share her husband's house, the rivalry of the mothers had threatened to extend to the children, the domesticity of home was destroyed, and its harmony was no longer possible. Then she left Oliel, and fled back to England, taking Israel with her.

Her father was dead, and the welcome she got of her half-brothers was not warm. They had no sympathy with her rebellion against her husband's second marriage. If she had married into a foreign country, she should abide by the ways of it. Sara was heartbroken. Her health had long been poor, and now it failed her utterly. In less than a month she died. On her death-bed she committed her boy to the care of her brothers, and implored them not to send him back to Morocco.

For years thereafter Israel's life in London was a stern one. If he had no longer to submit to the open contempt of the Moors, the kicks and insults of the streets, he had to learn how bitter is the bread that one is forced to eat at another's table. When he should have been still at school he was set to some menial occupation in the bank at Holborn Bars, and when he ought to have risen at his desk he was required to teach the sons of prosperous men the way to go above him. Life was playing an evil game with him, and, though he won, it must be at a bitter price.

Thus twelve years went by, and Israel, now three-and-twenty, was a tall, silent, very sedate young man, clear-headed on all subjects, and a master of figures. Never once during that time had his father written

to him, or otherwise recognised his existence, though
knowing of his whereabouts from the first by the
zealous importunities of his uncles. Then one day a
letter came, written in distant tone and formal manner
announcing that the writer had been some time con-
fined to his bed, and did not expect to leave it ; that
the children of his second wife had died in infancy :
that he was alone, and had no one of his own flesh
and blood to look to his business, which was therefore
in the hands of strangers, who robbed him ; and
finally, that if Israel felt any duty towards his father,
or, failing that, if he had any wish to consult his own
interest, he would lose no time in leaving England
for Morocco.

Israel read the letter without a throb of filial
affection ; but, nevertheless, he concluded to obey its
summons. A fortnight later he landed at Tangier.
He had come too late. His father had died the day
before. The weather was stormy, and the surf on the
shore was heavy, and thus it chanced that, even while
the crazy old packet on which he sailed lay all day

beating about the bay, in fear of being dashed on to the ruins of the mole, his father's body was being buried in the little Jewish cemetery outside the eastern walls, and his cousins, and cousins' cousins, to the fifth degree, without loss of time or waste of sentiment, were busily dividing his inheritance among them.

Next day, as his father's heir, he claimed from the Moorish court the restitution of his father's substance. But his cousins made the Kádi, the judge, a present of a hundred dollars, and he was declared to be an impostor, who could not establish his identity. Producing his father's letter which had summoned him from London, he appealed from the Kádi to the Âolámà, men wise in the law, who acted as referees in disputed cases; but it was decided that as a Jew he had no right in Mohammedan law to offer evidence in a civil court. He laid his case before the British Consul, but was found to have no claim to English intervention, being a subject of the Sultan both by birth and parentage. Meantime, his dispute with his cousins was set at rest for ever by the Governor of the town, who, concluding that his father had left neither will nor heirs, confiscated everything he had possessed to the public treasury—that is to say, to the Kaid's own uses.

Thus he found himself without standing ground in Morocco, whether as a Jew, a Moor, or an Englishman, a stranger in his father's country, and openly branded as a cheat. That he did not return to England promptly was because he was already a man of indomitable spirit. Besides that, the treatment he was having now was but of a piece with what he had received at all times. Nothing had availed to crush him, even as nothing ever does avail to crush a man of character. But the obstacles and torments which make no impression on the mind of a strong man often make a very sensible impression on his heart; the mind triumphs, it is the heart that suffers; the mind strengthens and expands after every besetting plague of life, but the heart withers and wears away.

So far from flying from Morocco when things conspired together to beat him down, Israel looked about with an equal mind for the means of settling there.

His opportunity came early. The Governor, either by qualm of conscience or further freak of selfishness, got him the place of head of the Oománà, the three Administrators of Customs at Tangier. He held the post six months only, to the complete satisfaction of the Kaid, but amid the muttered discontent of the merchants and tradesmen. Then the Governor of Tetuan, a bigger town lying a long day's journey to the east, hearing of Israel that as Ameen of Tangier he had doubled the custom revenues in half a year, invited him to fill an informal, unofficial, and irregular position as assessor of tributes.

Now, it would be a long task to tell of the work which Israel did in his new calling : how he regulated the market dues and appointed a Mut·hasseb, a clerk of the market, to collect them—so many moozoonahs for every camel sold, so many for every horse, mule and ass, so many floos for every fowl, and so many metkals for the purchase and sale of every slave ;

how he numbered the houses and made lists of the
trades, assessing their tribute by the value of their
businesses—so much for gun-making, so much for
weaving, so much for tanning, and so on through the
line of them, great and small, good and bad, even
from the trades of the Jewish silversmiths and the
Moorish packsaddle-makers down to the callings of
the Arab water-carriers and the ninety public
women.

All this he did by the strict law and letter of the
Koran, which entitled the Sultan to a tithe of all
earnings whatsoever; but it would not wrong the
truth to say that he did it, also, by the impulse of a
sour and saddened heart. The world had shown no
mercy to him, and he need show no mercy to the
world. Why talk of pity? It was only a name, an
idea, a mocking thought. In the actual reckoning of
life there was no such thing as pity. Thus did
Israel justify himself in all his dealings, whatever their severity and the rigour wherewith they
wrought.

And the people felt the strong hand that was on them, and they cursed it.

" Ya Allah! Allah!" the Moors would cry. "Who is this Jew—this son of the English—that he should be made our master?"

They muttered at him in the streets, they scowled upon him, and at length they insulted him openly. Since his return from England he had resumed the dress of his race in his country—the long dark kaftan, with a scarf for girdle, the black slippers, and the black skull-cap. And, going one day by the Grand Mosque, a group of the beggars, who lay always by the gate, called on him to uncover his feet.

"Jew! Dog!" they cried, "there is no god but God! Curses on your relations! Off with your slippers!"

He paid no heed to their commands, but made straight onward. Then one blear-eyed and scab-faced cripple scrambled up and struck off his cap with a crutch. He picked it up again without a look or a word, and strode away. But next morning, at early prayers, there was a place empty at the door of the mosque.   Its accustomed occupant lay in the prison at the Kasbah.

And if the Muselmeen hated Israel for what he was doing for their Governor, the Jews hated him yet more because it was being done for a Moor.

"He has sold himself to our enemy," they said, "against the welfare of his own nation."

At the synagogue they ignored him, and in taking the votes of their people they counted others and passed him by.   He showed no malice.   Only his strong face twitched at each fresh insult, and his head was held higher.   Only this, and one other sign of suffering in that secret place of his withering heart, which God's eye alone could see.

Thus far he had done no more to Moor and Jew than exact that tenth part of their substance which the faiths of both required that they should pay. But now his work went further.   A little group of old Jews, all held in honour among their people— Abraham Ohana, nicknamed Pigman, son of a former rabbi; Judah ben Lolo, an elder of his synagogue; and

Reuben Maliki, keeper of the poor-box—were seized and cast into the Kasbah for gross and base usury.

At this the Jewish quarter was thrown into wild hubbub. The hand that was on their people was a daring and terrible one. None doubted whose hand it was—it was the hand of young Israel the Jew.

When the three old usurers had bought themselves out of the Kasbah, they put their heads together and said, "Let us drive this fellow out of the Mellah, and so shall he be driven out of the town." Then the owner of the house which Israel rented for his lodging evicted him by a poor excuse, and all other Jewish owners refused him as tenant. But the conspiracy failed. By command of the Governor, or by his influence, Israel was lodged by the Nadir, the administrator of mosque property, in one of the houses belonging to the mosque on the Moorish side of the Mellah walls.

Seeing this, the usurers laid their heads together again, and said, "Let us see that no man of our nation serve him, and so shall his life be a burden." Then the two Jews who had been his servants deserted him, and when he asked for Moors he was told that the faithful might not obey the unbeliever; and when he would have sent for negroes out of the Soudan he was warned that a Jew might not hold a slave. But the conspiracy failed again. Two black female slaves from Soos, named Fatimah and Habeebah, were bought in the name of the Governor and assigned to Israel's service.

And when it was seen at length that nothing availed to disturb Israel's material welfare, the three base usurers laid their heads together yet again, that they might prey upon his superstitious fears, and they said, "He is our enemy, but he is a Jew: let the woman who is named the prophetess put her curse upon him." Then she who was so called, one Rebecca Bensabbot, deaf as a stone, weak in her intellect, seventy years of age, and living fifty years on the poor-box which Reuben Maliki kept, crossed Israel in the streets, and cursed him as a son of Beelzebub, predicting that, even as he had made the walls of the Kasbah to echo with the groans of God's elect, so should his own spirit be broken within them, and his forehead humbled to the earth. He stood while he heard her out, and his strong lip trembled at her words; but he only smiled coldly, and passed on in silence.

"The clouds are not hurt," he thought, "by the bark of dogs."

Thus did his brethren of Judah revile him, and thus did they torture him; yet there was one among them who did neither. This was the daughter of their Grand Rabbi, David ben Ohana. Her name was Ruth. She was young, and God had given her grace, and she was beautiful, and many young Jewish men of Tetuan had vied with each other in vain for her favour. Of Israel's duty she knew little, save what report had said of it, that it was evil, and of the acts which had made him an outcast among his own people, and an Ishmael among the sons of Ishmael, she could form no judgment. But what a woman's eyes might see in him, without help of other know ledge, that she saw.

She had marked him in the synagogue, that his face was noble and his manners gracious; that he was young, but only as one who had been cheated of his youth and had missed his early manhood; that when he was ignored he ignored his insult, and when he was reviled he answered not again; in a word, that he was silent and strong and alone, and, above all, that he was sad.

These were credentials enough to the true girl's favour, and Israel soon learnt that the house of the Rabbi was open to him. There the lonely man first found himself. The cold eyes of his little world had seen him only as his father's son, but the light and warmth of the eyes of Ruth saw him as the son of his mother also. The Rabbi himself was old, very old—ninety years of age—and length of days had taught him charity. And so it was that when, in due time, Israel came with many excuses and asked for Ruth in marriage, the Rabbi gave her to him.

The betrothal followed, but none save the notary and his witnesses stood beside Israel when he crossed hands over the handkerchief; and, when the marriage came in its course, few stood beside the Chief Rabbi. Nevertheless, all the Jews of the quarter and all the Moors of Tetuan were alive to what was happening, and on the night of the marriage a great company of both peoples, though chiefly of the rabble among them, gathered in front of the Rabbi's house that they might hiss and jeer.

The Chacham heard them from where he sat under the stars in his patio, and when at last the voice of Rebecca the prophetess came to him above the tumult, crying, "Woe to her that has married the enemy of her nation, and woe to him that gave her against the hope of his people! They shall taste death. He shall see them fall from his side and die," then the old man listened and trembled visibly. In confusion and fierce anger he rose up and stumbled through the crooked passage to the door, and flinging it wide he stood in the doorway, facing them that stood without.

"Peace! peace!" he cried, "and shame! shame!

Remember the doom of him that shall curse the high-priest of the Lord."

This he spoke in a voice that shook with wrath. Then suddenly, his voice failing him, he said in a broken whisper, " My good people, what is this ? Your servant is grown old in your service. Sixty and odd years he has shared your sorrows and your burdens. What has he done this day that your women should lift up their voices against him ? "

But, in awe of his white head in the moonlight, the rabble that stood in the darkness were silent and made no answer. Then he staggered back, and Israel helped him into his house, and Ruth did what she could to compose him. But he was wofully shaken, and that night he died.

When the Rabbi's death became known in the morning, the Jews whispered, " It is the first-fruits ! " and the Moors touched their foreheads and murmured, " It is written ! "

CHAPTER II.

ISRAEL paid no heed to Jew or Moor, but in due time he set about the building of a house for himself and for Ruth, that they might live in comfort many years together. In the south-east corner of the Mellah he placed it, and he built it partly in the Moorish and partly in the English fashion, with an open court and corridors, marble pillars, and a marble staircase, walls of small tiles, and ceilings of stalactites, but also with windows and with doors. And when his house was raised he put no haities into it, and spread no mattresses on the floors, but sent for tables and chairs and couches out of England; and everything he did in this wise cut him off the more from the people about him, both Moors and Jews.

And being settled at last, and his own master in

his own dwelling, out of the power of his enemies to push him back into the streets, suddenly it smote him for the first time that whereas the house he had built was a refuge for himself, it was doomed to be little better than a prison for his wife. In marrying Ruth he had enlarged the circle of his intimates by one faithful and loving soul; but, in marrying him, she had reduced even her friends to that number. Her father was dead; if she was the daughter of a Chief Rabbi she was also the wife of an outcast, the companion of a pariah, and, save for him, she must be for ever alone. Even their bondwomen still spoke a foreign dialect, and commerce with them was mainly by signs.

Thinking of all this with some remorse, one idea fixed itself on Israel's mind, one hope on his heart—that Ruth might soon bear a child. Then would her solitude be broken by the dearest company that a woman might know on earth. And, if he had wronged her, his child would make amends.

Israel thought of this again and again. The

delicious hope pursued him. It was his secret, and he never gave it speech. But time passed, and no child was born. And Ruth herself saw that she was barren, and she began to cast down her head before her husband. Israel's hope was of longer life, but the truth dawned upon him at last. Then, when he saw that his wife was ashamed, a great tenderness came over him. He had been thinking of her, that a child would bring her solace, and meanwhile she had thought only of him, that a child would be his pride. After that he never went abroad but he came home with stories of women wailing at the cemetery over the tombs of their babes, of men broken in heart for loss of their sons, and of how they were best treated of God who were given no children.

This served his big soul for a time to cheat it of its disappointment, half deceiving Ruth, and deceiving himself entirely. But one day the woman Rebecca met him again at the street-corner by his own house, and she lifted her gaunt finger into his face, and cried, "Israel ben Oliel, the judgment of the Lord is upon you, and will not suffer you to raise up children to be a reproach and a curse among your people!"

"Out upon you, woman!" cried Israel, and almost in the first delirium of his pain he had lifted his hand to strike her. Her other predictions had passed him by, but this one had smitten him. He went home and shut himself in his room, and throughout that day he let no one come near to him.

Israel knew his own heart at last. At his wife's barrenness he was now angry with the anger of a proud man whose pride had been abased. What was the worth of it, after all, that he had conquered the fate that had first beaten him down? What did it come to that the world was at his feet? Heaven was above him, and the poorest man in the Mellah who was the father of a child might look down on him with contempt.

That night sleep forsook his eyelids, and his mouth was parched and his spirit bitter. And sometimes he reproached himself with a thousand offences, and sometimes he searched the Scriptures, that he might persuade himself that he had walked blameless before the Lord in the ordinances and commandments of God.

Meantime, Ruth, in her solitude, remembered that it was now three years since she had been married to Israel, and that by the laws both of their race and their country a woman who had been long barren might straightway be divorced by her husband.

Next morning a message of business came from the Khaleefa, but Israel would not answer it. Then came an order to him from the Governor, but still he paid no heed. At length he heard a feeble knock at the door of his room. It was Ruth, his wife, and he opened to her and she entered.

"Send me away from you!" she cried. "Send me away!"

"Not for the place of the Kaid," he answered stoutly; "no, nor the throne of the Sultan!"

At that she fell on his neck and kissed him, and they mingled their tears together. But he comforted her at length, and said, "Look up, my dearest! look up! I am a proud man among men, but it is even as the Lord may deal with me. And which of us shall murmur against God?"

At that word Ruth lifted her head from his bosom, and her eyes were full of a sudden thought.

"Then let us ask of the Lord," she whispered hotly, "and surely He will hear our prayer."

"It is the voice of the Lord Himself!" cried Israel; "and this day it shall be done!"

At the time of evening prayers Israel and Ruth went up hand in hand, together to the synagogue, in a narrow lane, off the Sôk el Fóki. And Ruth knelt in her place in the gallery close under the iron grating and the candles that hung above it, and she prayed: "O Lord, have pity on this Thy servant, and take away her reproach among women. Give her grace in Thine eyes, O Lord, that her husband be not ashamed. Grant her a child of Thy mercy, that his eye may smile upon her. Yet not as she willeth, but as Thou willest, O Lord, and Thy servant will be satisfied."

But Israel stood long on the floor with his hand on his heart and his eyes to the ground, and he called on God as a debtor that will not be appeased, saying: "How long wilt Thou forget me, O Lord? My enemies triumph over me and foretell Thy doom upon me. They sit in the lurking-places of the streets to deride me. Confound my enemies, O Lord, and rebuke their counsels. Remember Ruth, I beseech Thee, that she is patient and her heart is humbled. Give her children of Thy servant, and her first-born shall be sanctified unto Thee. Give her one child, and it shall be Thine—if it is a son, to be a Rabbi in Thy synagogues. Hear me, O Lord, and give heed to my cry, for behold I swear it before Thee. One child, but one, only one, son or daughter, and all my desire is before Thee. How long wilt Thou forget me, O Lord?"

Now, the message of the Khaleefa which Israel had not answered in his trouble was a request from the Shereef of Wazzán that he should come without delay to that town to count his rent-charges and assess his dues. This request the Governor had transformed into a command, for the Shereef was a prince of Islam in his own country, and in many provinces the believers paid him tribute. So in three days' time Israel was ready to set forth on his journey, with men and mules at his door, and camels packed with tents.

He was likely to be some months absent from Tetuan, and it was impossible that Ruth should go with him. They had never been separated before, and Ruth's concern was that they should be so long parted, but Israel's was a deeper matter.

"Ruth," he said, when his time came, " I am going away from you, but my enemies remain. They see evil in all my doings, and in this act also they will find offence. Promise me that if they make a mock at you, for your husband's sake you will not see them ; if they taunt you that you will not hear them ; and if they ask anything concerning me that you will answer them not at all."

And Ruth promised him that if his enemies made a mock at her she should be as one that was blind, if they taunted her as one that was deaf, and if they questioned her concerning her husband as one that was dumb. Then they parted with many tears and embraces.

Israel was half a year absent in the town and province of Wazzán, and, having finished the work which he came to do, he was sent back to Tetuan loaded with presents from the Shereef, and surrounded by soldiers and attendants, who did not leave him until they had brought him to the door of his own house.

And there, in her chamber, sat Ruth awaiting him, her eyes dim with tears of joy. her throat throbbing like the throat of a bird, and great news on her tongue. The prayer in the synagogue had been heard, and the child they had asked for was to come.

Israel was like a man beside himself with joy. He burst in upon the message of his wife, and caught her to his breast again and again, and kissed her. Long they stood together so, while he told her of the chances which had befallen him during his absence from her, and she told him of her solitude of six long months, unbroken save for the poor company of

Fatimah and Habeebah, wherein she had been blind and deaf and dumb to all the world.

During the months thereafter until Ruth's time was full Israel sat with her constantly. He could scarce suffer himself to leave her company. He covered her chamber with fruits and flowers. There was no desire of her heart but he fulfilled it. And they talked together lovingly of how they would name the child when the time came to name it. Israel concluded that if it was a son it should be called David, and Ruth decided that if it was a daughter it should be called Naomi. And Ruth delighted to tell of how when it was weaned she should take it up to the synagogue, and say : "O Lord ! I am the woman that knelt before Thee praying. For this child I prayed, and Thou hast heard my prayer." And Israel told of how his son should grow up to be a Rabbi to minister before God, and how in those days it should come to pass that the children of his father's enemies should crouch to him for a piece of silver and a morsel of bread. Thus they built themselves castles in the air for the future of the child that was to come.

Ruth's time came at last, and it was also the time of the Feast of the Passover, being in the month of Nisan. This was a cause of joy to Israel, for he was eager to triumph over his enemies face to face, and he could not wait eight other days for the Feast of the Circumcision. So, he set a supper fit for a king: the fore-leg of a sheep and the fore-leg of an ox, the egg roasted in ashes, the balls of Charoseth, the three Mitzvoth, and the wine. And by the time the supper was ready the midwife had been summoned, and it was the day of the night of the Seder.

Then Israel sent messengers round the Mellah to summon his guests. Only his enemies he invited, his bitterest foes, his unceasing revilers, and among them were the three base usurers, Abraham Pigman, Judah ben Lolo, and Reuben Maliki. " They cursed me," he thought, " and I shall look on their con-fusion." His heart thirsted to summon Rebecca

Bensabbot also, but well he knew that her dainty masters would not sit at meat with her.

And when the enemies were bidden, all of them excused themselves and refused, saying it was the Feast of the Passover, when no man should sit save in his own house, and at his own table. But Israel was not to be gainsaid. He went out to them himself, and said, " Come, let bygones be bygones. It is the feast of our nation. Let us eat and drink together." So, partly by his importunity, but mainly in their bewilderment, yet against all rule and custom, they suffered themselves to go with him.

And when they were come into his house and were seated about his table in the patio, and he had washed his hands and taken the wine and blessed it, and passed it to all, and they had drunk together, he could not keep back his tongue from taunting them. Then when he had washed again and dipped the celery in the vinegar, and they had drunk of the wine once more, he taunted them afresh and laughed. But nothing yet had they understood of his meaning, and they looked into each other's faces and asked, "What is it?"

"Wait! Only wait!" Israel answered. "You shall see!"

At that moment Ruth sent for him to her chamber and he went in to her.

"I am a sorrowful woman," she said. "Some evil is about to befall—I know it, I feel it."

But he only rallied her and laughed again, and prophesied joy on the morrow. Then, returning to the patio, where the passover cakes had been broken, he called for the supper, and bade his guests to eat and drink as much as their hearts desired.

They could do neither now, for the fear that possessed them at sight of Israel's frenzy. The three old usurers, Abraham, Judah, and Reuben, rose to go, but Israel cried, "Stay! Stay, and see what is to come!" and under the very force of his will they yielded and sat down again.

Still Israel drank and laughed and derided them. In the wild torrent of his madness he called them by names they knew and by names they did not know —Harpagon, Shylock, Bildad, Elihu—and at every new name he laughed again. And while he carried himself so in the outer court the slave woman Fatimah came from the inner room with word that the child was born.

At that Israel was like a man distraught. He leapt up from the table and faced full upon his guests, and cried, "Now you know what it is; and now you know why you are bidden to this supper! You are here to rejoice with me over my enemies! Drink! drink! Confusion to all of them!" And he lifted a winecup and drank himself.

They were abashed before him, and tried to edge out of the patio into the street; but he put his back to the passage, and faced them again.

"You will not drink?" he said. "Then listen to me." He dashed the winecup out of his hand, and it broke into fragments on the floor. His laughter was gone, his face was aflame, and his voice

rose to a shrill cry. "You foretold the doom of
God upon me, you brought me low, you made me
ashamed: but behold how the Lord has lifted me
up! You set your women to prophesy that God
would not suffer me to raise up children to be a
reproach and a curse among my people; but God
has this day given me a son like the best of you.
More than that—more than that—my son shall yet
see——"

The slave woman was touching his arm. "It is a
girl," she said; "a girl!"

For a moment Israel stammered and paused.
Then he cried: "No matter! She shall see your
own children fatherless, and with none to show them
mercy! She shall see the iniquity of their fathers
remembered against them! She shall see them beg
their bread, and seek it in desolate places! And
now you can go! Go! go!"

He had stepped aside as he spoke, and with a
sweep of his arm he was driving them all out like
sheep before him, dumbfounded and with their eyes

in the dust, when suddenly there was a low cry from the inner room.

It was Ruth calling for her husband. Israel wheeled about and went in to her hurriedly, and his enemies, by one impulse of evil instinct, followed him and listened from the threshold.

Ruth's face was a face of fear, and her lips moved, but no voice came from them.

And Israel said : " How is it with you, my dearest, joy of my joy and pride of my pride ? "

Then Ruth lifted the babe from her bosom and said : " The Lord has counted my prayer to me as sin—look, see, the child is both dumb and blind ! "

At that word Israel's heart died within him, but he muttered out of his dry throat, " No, no, never believe it ! "

" True, true, it is true," she moaned, " the child has not uttered a cry, and its eyelids have not blinked at the light."

" Never believe it, I say ! " Israel growled, and he lifted the babe in his arms to try it.

But when he held it to the fading light of the window which opened upon the street where the woman called the prophetess had cursed him, the eyes of the child did not close, neither did their pupils diminish. Then his limbs began to tremble, so that the midwife took the babe out of his arms and laid it again on its mother's bosom.

And Ruth wept over it, saying, "Even if it were a son never could it serve in the synagogue! Never! Never!"

At that Israel began to curse and to swear. His enemies had now pushed themselves into the chamber, and they cried, "Peace! Peace!" And old Judah ben Lolo, the elder of the synagogue, grunted, and said, "Is it not written that no one afflicted of God shall minister in His temples?"

Israel stared around in silence into the faces about him, first into the face of his wife and then into the faces of his enemies whom he had bidden. Then he fell to laughing hideously and crying, "What matter? Every monkey is a gazelle to

its mother ?"　But after that he staggered, his knees
gave way. he pitched half forward and half aside,
like a falling horse, and with a deep groan he fell
with his face to the floor.

The midwife and the slave lifted him up and
moistened his lips with water; but his enemies
turned and left him, muttering among themselves,
" The Lord killeth and maketh alive, He bringeth
low and lifteth up, and into the pit that the evil
man diggeth for another He causeth his foot to
slip."

CHAPTER III.

THROUGHOUT Tetuan and the country round about, Israel was now an object of contempt. God had declared against him, God had brought him low, God Himself had filled him with confusion. Then why should man show him mercy?

But if he was despised he was still powerful. None dare openly insult him. And, between their fear and their scorn of him, the shifts of the rabble to give vent to their contempt were often ludicrous enough. Thus, they would call their dogs and their asses by his name, and the dogs would be the scabbiest in the streets, and the asses the laziest in the markets.

He would be caught in the crush of the traffic at the town gate or at the gate of the Mellah, and while he stood aside to allow a line of pack-mules to pass he would hear a voice from behind him crying huskily, "Accursed old Israel! Get on home to your mother!" Then, turning quickly round, he would find that close at his heels a negro of most innocent countenance was cudgelling his donkey by that title.

He would go past the Saints' Houses in the public ways, and at the sound of his footstep the bleached and eyeless lepers who sat under the white walls, crying "Allah! Allah! Allah!" would suddenly change their cry to "Arrah! Arrah! Arrah!" "Go on! Go on! Go on!"

He would walk across the Sôk on Fridays, and hear shrieks and peals of laughter, and see grinning faces with gleaming white teeth turned in his direction, and he would know that the story-tellers were mimicking his voice and the jugglers imitating his gestures.

His prosperity counted for nothing against the open brand of God's displeasure. The veriest muck-worm in the market-place spat out at sight of him.

Moor and Jew, Arab and Berber—they all despised him !

Nevertheless, the disaster which had befallen his house had not crushed him. It had brought out every fibre of his being, every muscle of his soul. He had quarrelled with God by reason of it, and his quarrel with God had made his quarrel with his fellow-man the fiercer.

There was just one man in the town who found no offence in either form of warfare. The more wicked the one and the more outrageous the other, the better for this person.

It was the Governor of Tetuan. His name was El î Arby, but he was known as Ben Aboo, the son of his father. That father had been none other than the late Sultan. Therefore Ben Aboo was a brother of Abd er-Rahman, though by another mother, a negro slave. To be a Sultan's brother in Morocco is not to be a Sultan's favourite, but a possible aspirant to his throne. Nevertheless Ben Aboo had been made a Kaid, a chief, in the Sultan's army, and eventually a

commander-in-chief of his cavalry. In that capacity
he had led a raid for arrears of tribute on the Beni
Hasan, the Beni Idar, and the Wad Ras. These rebellious tribes inhabit the country near to Tetuan,
and hence Ben Aboo's attention had been first directed
to that town. When he had returned from his ex-
pedition he offered the Sultan fifteen thousand
dollars for the place of its Basha, or Governor, and
promised him thirty thousand dollars a year as
tribute. The Sultan took his money, and accepted
his promise. There was a Basha at Tetuan already,
but that was a trifling difficulty. The good man was
summoned to the Sultan's presence, accused of
appropriating the Shereefian tributes, stripped of all
he had, and cast into prison.

That was how Ben Aboo had become Governor of
Tetuan, and the story of how Israel had become his
informal Administrator of Affairs is no less curious.
At first Ben Aboo seemed likely to lose by his dubious
transaction. His new function was partly military
and partly civil. He was a valiant soldier—the black

blood of his slave-mother had counted for so much ;
but he was a bad administrator—he could neither
read nor write nor reckon figures.   In this dilemma
his natural colleague would have been his Khaleefa,
his deputy, Ali bin Jillool, but because this man had
been the deputy of his predecessor also, he could not
trust him.   He had two other immediate subordin-
ates, his Commander of Artillery and his Commander
of Infantry, but neither of them could spell the letters
of his name.   Then there was his Táleb the Ádel, his
scribe the notary, Hosain ben Hashen, styled Haj,
because he had made the pilgrimage to Mecca, but
he was also the Imâm, or head of the Mosque, and
the wily Ben Aboo foresaw the danger of some day
coming into collision with the religious sentiment of
his people.   Finally, there was the Kadi, Mohammed
ben Arly, but the judge was an official outside his
jurisdiction, and he wanted a man who should be
under his hand.   That was the combination of cir-
cumstances whereby Israel came to Tetuan.

Israel's first years in his strange office had satisfied

his master entirely. He had carried the Basha's seal
and acted for him in all affairs of money. The
revenues had risen to fifty thousand dollars, so that
the Basha had twenty thousand to the good. Then
Ben Aboo's ambition began to override itself. He
started an oil-mill, and wanted Israel to select a
hundred houses owned by rich men, that he
might compel each house to take ten kollahs of oil
—an extravagant quantity, at seven dollars for each
kollah—an exorbitant price. Israel had refused.
" It is not just," he had said.

Other expedients for enlarging his revenue Ben
Aboo had suggested, but Israel had steadfastly re-
sisted all of them. Sometimes the Governor had
pretended that he had received an order from the
Sultan to impose a gross and wicked tax, but Israel's
answer had been the same. " There is no evil in
the world but injustice," he had said. " Do justice,
and you do all that God can ask or man expect."

For such opposition to the will of the Basha any
other person would have been cast into a damp

dungeon at night, and chained in the hot sun by day. Israel was still necessary. So Ben Aboo merely longed for the dawn of that day whereon he should need him no more.

But since the disaster which had befallen Israel's house everything had undergone a change. It was now Israel himself who suggested dubious means of revenue. There was no device of a crafty brain for turning the very air itself into money—ransoms, promissory notes, and false judgments—but Israel thought of it. Thus he persuaded the Governor to send his small currency to the Jewish shops to be changed into silver dollars at the rate of nine ducats to the dollar, when a dollar was worth ten in currency. And after certain of the shopkeepers, having changed fifty thousand dollars at that rate, fled to the Sultan to complain, Israel advised that their debtors should be called together, their debts purchased, and bonds drawn up and certified for ten times the amounts of them. Thus a few were banished from their homes in fear of imprisonment,

many were sorely harassed, and some were entirely
ruined.

It was a strange spectacle. He whom the rabble
gibed at in the public streets held the fate of every
man of them in his hand. Their dogs and their
asses might bear his name, but their own lives and
liberty must answer to it.

Israel looked on at all with an equal mind, neither
flinching at his indignities nor glorying in his power.
He beheld the wreck of families without remorse, and
heard the wail of women and the cry of children
without a qualm. Neither did he delight in the
sufferings of them that had derided him. His evil
impulse was a higher matter—his faith in justice
had been broken up. He had been wrong. There
there was no such thing as justice in the world, and
there could, therefore, be no such thing as injustice.
There was nothing but the blind swirl of chance, and
the wild scramble for life. The man had quarrelled
with God.

But Israel's heart was not yet dead. There was

one place, where he who bore himself with such austerity towards the world was a man of great tenderness. That place was his own home. What he saw there was enough to stir the fountains of his being—nay, to exhaust them, and to send him abroad as a river-bed that is dry.

In that first hour of his abasement, after he had been confounded before the enemies whom he had expected to confound, Israel had thought of himself, but Ruth's unselfish heart had even then thought only of the babe.

The child was born blind and dumb and deaf. At the feast of life there was no place left for it. So Ruth turned her face from it to the wall, and called on God to take it.

"Take it!" she cried—"take it! Make haste, O God, make haste and take it!"

But the child did not die. It lived and grew strong. Ruth herself suckled it, and as she nourished it in her bosom her heart yearned over it, and she forgot the prayer she had prayed concerning it. So,

littlo by little, her spirit returned to her, and day by
day her soul deceived her, and hour by hour an angel
out of heaven seemed to come to her side and whisper,
" Take heart of hope, O Ruth !   God does not afflict
willingly.   Perhaps the child is not blind, perhaps
it is not deaf, perhaps it is not dumb.   Who shall
yet say ?   Wait and see ! "

And, during the first few months of its life, Ruth
could see no difference in her child from the children
of other women.   Sometimes she would kneel by its
cradle and gaze into the flower-cup of its eye, and
the eye was blue and beautiful, and there was nothing
to say that the little cup was broken, and the little
chamber dark.   And sometimes she would look at
the pretty shell of its ear, and the ear was round and
full as a shell on the shore, and nothing told her that
the voice of the sea was not heard in it, and that all
within was silence.

So Ruth cherished her hope in secret, and whispered her heart and said, " It is well, all is well with
the child.   She will look upon my face and see it,

and listen to my voice and hear it, and her own little tongue will yet speak to me, and make me very glad." And then an ineffable serenity would spread over her face and transfigure it.

But when the time was come that a child's eyes, having grown familiar with the light, should look on its little hands, and stare at its little fingers, and clutch at its cradle, and gaze about in a peaceful per-plexity at everything, still the eyes of Ruth's child did not open in seeing, but lay idle and empty. And when the time was ripe that a child's ears should hear from hour to hour the sweet babble of a mother's love, and its tongue begin to give back the words in lisping sounds, the ear of Ruth's child heard nothing, and its tongue was mute.

Then Ruth's spirit sank, but still the angel out of heaven seemed to come to her, and find her a thou-sand excuses, and say, " Wait, Ruth ; only wait, only a little longer."

So Ruth held back her tears, and bent above her babe again, and watched for its smile that should answer to her smile, and listened for the prattle of its little lips. But never a sound as of speech seemed to break the silence between the words that trembled from her own tongue, and never once across her baby's face passed the light of her tearful smile.

It was a pitiful thing to see her wasted pains, and most pitiful of all for the pains she was at to conceal them. Thus, every day at midday she would carry her little one into the patio, and watch if its eyes should blink in the sunshine; but if Israel chanced to come upon her then, she would drop her head and say, "How sweet the air is to-day, and how pleasant to sit in the sun!"

Thus, too, when a bird was singing from the fig-tree that grew in the court, she would catch up her child and carry it close, and watch if its ears should hear; but if Israel saw her, she would laugh—a little shrill laugh like a cry—and cover her face in confusion.

For a time Israel tried to humour her, seeming not to see what he saw, and pretending not to hear what he heard. But every day his heart bled at sight of her, and one day he could bear up no longer, for his very soul had sickened, and he cried, "Have done, Ruth!—for mercy's sake, have done! The child is a soul in chains, and a spirit in prison. Her eyes are darkness, like the tomb's, and her ears are silence, like the grave's. Never will she smile to her mother's smile, or answer to her father's speech. The first sound she will hear will be the last trump, and the first face she will see will be the face of God."

At that, Ruth flung herself down and burst into a flood of tears. The hope that she had cherished was dead. Israel could comfort her no longer. The fountain of his own·heart was dry. He drew a long breath, and went away to his bad work at the Kasbah.

The child lived and thrived. They had called her Naomi, as they had agreed to do before she was born, though no name she knew of herself, and a mockery it seemed to name her. At four years of age she was a creature of the most delicate beauty. Notwithstanding her Jewish parentage, she was fair as the day and fresh as the dawn. And if her eyes were darkness, there was light within her soul; and if her ears were silence, there was music within her heart. She was brighter than the sun which she could not see, and sweeter than the songs which she could not hear. She was joyous as a bird in its narrow cage, and never did she fret at the bars which bound her. And, like the bird that sings at midnight, her cheery soul sang in its darkness.

Only one sound seemed ever to come from her little lips, and it was the sound of laughter. With this she lay down to sleep at night, and rose again in the morning. She laughed as she combed her hair, and laughed again as she came dancing out of her chamber at dawn.

She had only one sentinel on the outpost of her spirit, and that was the sense of touch and feeling. With this she seemed to know the day from the night, and when the sun was shining and when the sky was dark. She knew her mother, too, by the

touch of her fingers, and her father by the brushing
of his beard. She knew the flowers that grew in the
fields outside the gate of the town, and she would
gather them in her lap, as other children did, and
bring them home with her in her hands. She
seemed almost to know their colours also, for the
flowers which she would twine in her hair were red,
and the white were those which she would lay on her
bosom. And truly a flower she was of herself,
whereto the wind alone could whisper, and only the
sun could speak aloud.

Sweet and touching were the efforts she sometimes
made to cling to them that were about her. Thus
her heart was the heart of a child, and she knew no
delight like to that of playing with other children.
But her father's house was under a ban; no child of
any neighbour in Tetuan was allowed to cross its
threshold, and, save for the children whom she met
in the fields when she walked there by her mother's
hand, no child did she ever meet.

Ruth saw this, and then, for the first time, she

became conscious of the isolation in which she had lived since her marriage with Israel. She herself had her husband for companion and comrade, but her little Naomi was doubly and trebly alone—first, alone as a child that is the only child of her parents; again, alone as a child whose parents are cut off from the parents of other children; and yet again, once more, alone as a child that is blind and dumb.

But Israel saw it also, and one day he brought home with him from the Kasbah a little black boy with a sweet round face and big innocent white eyes which might have been the eyes of an angel. The boy's name was Ali, and he was four years old. His father had killed his mother for infidelity and neglect of their child, and, having no one to buy him out of prison, he had that day been executed. Then little Ali had been left all alone in the world, and so Israel had taken him.

Ruth welcomed the boy, and adopted him. He had been born a Mohammedan, but secretly she brought him up as a Jew. And for some years thereafter no difference did she make between him and her own child that other eyes could see. They ate together, they walked abroad together, they played together, they slept together, and the little black head of the boy lay with the fair head of the girl on the same white pillow.

Strange and pathetic were the relations between these little exiles of humanity! One knew not whether to laugh or cry at them. First, on Ali's part, a blank wonderment that when he cried to Naomi, "Come!" she did not hear, when he asked, "Why?" she did not answer, and when he said "Look!" she did not see, though her blue eyes seemed to gaze full into his face. Then, a sort of amused bewilderment that her little nervous fingers were always touching his arms and his hands, and his neck and his throat. But long before he had come to know that Naomi was not as he was, that Nature had not given her eyes to see as he saw, and ears to hear as he heard, and a tongue to speak as he spoke, Nature herself had overstepped the barriers that divided her from him. He found that Naomi had come to understand him, whatever in his little way he did, and almost whatever in his little way he said. So he played with her as he would have played with any other playmate, laughing with her, calling to her, and going through his foolish little boyish antics before her. Nevertheless, by some mysterious knowledge of Nature's own teaching, he seemed to realise that it was his duty to take care of her. And when the spirit and the mischief in his little manly heart would prompt him to steal out of the house, and adventure into the streets with Naomi by his side, he would be found in the thick of the throng, perhaps at the heels of the mules and asses, with Naomi's hand locked in his hand, trying to push the great creatures of the crowd from before her, and crying in his brave little treble, " Arrah ! " " Ar-rah !" " Ar r-ah ! "

As for Naomi, the coming of little black Ali was a wild delight to her. Whatever Ali did, that would she do also. If he ran she would run ; if he sat she

would sit; and meanwhile she would laugh with a
heart of glee, though she heard not what he said,
and saw not what he did, and knew not what he
meant. At the time of the harvest, when Ruth
took them out into the fields, she would ride on
Ali's back, and snatch at the ears of barley and leap
in her seat and laugh, yet nothing would she see of
the yellow corn, and nothing would she hear of the
song of the reapers, and nothing would she know of
the cries of Ali, who shouted to her while he ran,
forgetting in his playing that she heard him not.
And at night, when Ruth put them to bed in their
little chamber, and Ali knelt with his face towards
Jerusalem, Naomi would kneel beside him with a
reverent air, and all her laughter would be gone.
Then, as he prayed his prayer, her little lips would
move as if she were praying too, and her little hands
would be clasped together, and her little eyes would
be upraised.

Pretty and piteous sights! Who could look on
them without tears? One thing at least was clear:

if the soul of this child was in prison, nevertheless it was alive; and if it was in chains, nevertheless it could not die, but was immortal and unmaimed, and waited only for the hour when it should be linked to other souls, soul to soul in the chains of speech. But the years went on, and Naomi grew in beauty and increased in sweetness, but no angel came down to open the darkened windows of her eyes, and draw aside the heavy curtains of her ears.

CHAPTER IV.

FOR all her joy and all her prettiness, Naomi was a burden which only love could bear. To think of the girl by day, and to dream of her by night, never to sit by her without pity of her helplessness, and never to leave her without dread of the mischances that might so easily befall, to see for her, to hear for her, to speak for her, truly the tyranny of the burden was terrible.

Ruth sank under it. Through seven years she was eyes of the child's eyes, and ears of her ears, and tongue of her tongue. After that her own sight became dim, and her hearing faint. It was almost as if she had spent them on Naomi in the yearning of love and pity. Soon afterwards her bodily strength failed her also, and then she knew that her time had come, and that she was to lay down her burden for ever. But her burden had become dear, and she clung to it. She could not look upon the child and think it, that she, who had spent her strength for her from the first, must leave her now to other love and tending. So she betook herself to an upper room, and gave strict orders to Fatimah and Habeebah that Naomi was to be kept from her altogether, that sight of the child's helpless happy face might tempt her soul no more.

And there in her death-chamber Israel sat with her constantly, settling his countenance steadfastly, and coming and going softly. He was more constant than a slave, and more tender than a woman. His love was great, but also he was eating out his big heart with remorse. The root of his trouble was the child. He never talked of her, and neither did Ruth dwell upon her name. Yet they thought of little else while they sat together.

And even if they had been minded to talk of the child, what had they to say of her? They had no memories to recall, no sweet childish sayings, no

simple broken speech, no pretty lisp—nothing had
they to bring back out of any harvest of the past of
all the dear delicious wealth that lies stored in the
treasure-houses of the hearts of happy parents. That
way everything was a waste. Always, as Israel
entered her room, Ruth would say, "How is the
child?" And always Israel would answer, "She is
well." But, if at that moment Naomi's laughter
came up to them from the patio, where she played
with Ali, they would cover their faces and be silent.

It was a melancholy parting. No one came near
them—neither Moor nor Jew, neither Rabbi nor
elder. The idle women of the Mellah would sometimes stand outside in the street and look up at their
house, knowing that the black camel of death was
kneeling at their gate. Other company they had
none. In such solitude they passed four weeks, and
when the time of the end seemed near, Israel himself
read aloud the prayer for the dying, the prayer
Shema' Yisrael, and Ruth repeated the words of it
after him.

Meantime, while Ruth lay in the upper chamber, little Naomi sported and played in the patio with Ali, but she missed her mother constantly. This she made plain by many silent acts of helpless love that knew no way to speak aloud. Thus she would lay flowers on the seats where her mother had used to sit, and, if at night she found them untouched where she had left them, her little face would fall, and her laughter die off her lips; but if they had withered and some one had cast them into the oven, she would laugh again and fetch other flowers from the fields, until the house would be full of the odour of the meadow and the scent of the hill.

And well they knew, who looked upon her then, whom she missed, and what the question was that halted on her tongue; yet how could they answer her? There was no way to do that until she herself knew how to ask.

But this she did on a day near to the end. It was evening, and she was being put to bed by Habeebah, and had just risen from her innocent pantomime of prayer beside Ali, when Israel, coming from Ruth's chamber, entered the children's room. Then, touching with her hand the seat whereon Ruth had used to sit, Naomi laid down her head on the pillow, and then rose and lay down again, and rose yet again and yet again lay down, and then came to where Israel was and stood before him. And at that Israel knew that the soul of his helpless child had asked him, as plainly as words of the tongue can speak, how often she should lie to sleep at night and rise to play in the morning before her mother came to her again.

The tears gushed into his eyes, and he left the children and returned to his wife's chamber.

" Ruth," he cried, " call the child to you, I beseech you !"

" No, no, no !" cried Ruth.

" Let her come to you and touch you and kiss you, and be with you before it is too late," said Israel. " She misses you, and fills the house with flowers for you. It breaks my heart to see her."

" It will break mine also," said Ruth.

But she consented that Naomi should be called, and Fatimah was sent to fetch her.

The sun was setting, and through the window which looked out to the west, over the river and the orange orchards and the palpitating plains beyond, its dying rays came into the room in a bar of golden light. It fell at that instant on Ruth's face, and she was white and wasted. And through the other window of the room, which looked out over the Mellah into the town, and across the market-place to the mosque and to the battery on the hill, there came up from the darkening streets below the shuffle of the feet of a crowd and the sound of many voices. The Jews of Tetuan were trooping back to their own little quarter, that their Moorish masters might lock them into it for the night.

Naomi was already in bed, and Fatimah brought her away in her nightdress. She seemed to know where she was to be taken, for she laughed as Fatimah held her by the hand, and danced as she was led to her mother's chamber. But when she was come to the door of it, suddenly her laughter ceased, and her little face sobered, as if something in the close abode of pain had troubled the senses that were left to her.

It is, perhaps, the most touching experience of the deaf and blind that no greeting can ever welcome them. When Naomi stood like a little white vision at the threshold of the room, Israel took her hand in silence, and drew her up to the pillow of the bed where her mother rested, and in silence Ruth brought the child to her bosom.

Then a strange thing happened. For a moment Naomi seemed to be perplexed. She touched her mother's fingers, and they were changed, for they had grown thin and long. Then she felt her face, and that was changed also, for it was become withered and cold. And, missing the grasp of the one and the smile of the other, she first turned her little head aside as one that listens closely, and then gently withdrew herself from the arms that held her.

Ruth had watched her with eyes that overflowed, and now she burst into sobs outright.

"The child does not know me!" she cried. "Did I not tell you it would break my heart?"

"Try her again," said Israel; "try her again."

Ruth devoured her tears, and called on Fatimah to bring the child back to her side. Then, loosening the necklace that was about her own neck, she bound it about the neck of Naomi, and also the bracelets that were on her wrists she unclasped and clasped them on the wrists of the child. This she did that Naomi might remember the hands that had been kind to her always. But when the child felt the ornaments she seemed only to know, by the quick instinct of a girl, that she was decked out bravely, and giving no thought to Ruth, who waited and watched for the grasp of recognition and the kiss of joy, she withdrew herself again from her mother's arms, and bounded into the middle of the room, and suddenly began to laugh and to dance.

It was an awful thing to look upon in that still

hour. The sun's dying light, which had rested on Ruth's wasted face, now glistened and sparkled on the jewels of the child, and glowed on her blind eyes, and gleamed on her fair hair, and reddened her white nightdress while she danced and laughed to her mother's death. Nothing did the child know of death, any more than Adam himself before Abel was slain, and it was almost as if a devil out of hell had entered into her innocent heart, and possessed it that she might make a mock of the dying of the dearest friend she had known on earth.

It was a weird dream, a terrible nightmare, a consuming horror. On and on she danced, to no measure and no time, and not with a child's uncertain step which breaks down at motion as its tongue breaks down at speech, but wildly and deliriously. The room was darkening fast, but still across the nether end, by the foot of the bed, streamed the dull red bar of sunlight with the little red figure leaping and prancing and laughing in the midst of it.

With an awful cry Ruth fell back on the pillow
and turned her eyes to the wall. The black woman
dropped her head that she might not see. And
Israel covered his face and groaned in his tearless
agony, " O Lord God, long hast thou chastised me
with whips, and now I am chastised with scorpions!"

Ruth recovered herself quickly. " Bring her to
me again!" she faltered; and once more Fatimah
brought Naomi back to the bedside. Then, em-
bracing and kissing the child, and seeming to forget
in the torment of her trouble that Naomi could not
hear her, she cried, " It's your mother, Naomi!
your mother, darling, though so sick and changed!
Don't you know her, Naomi? Your mother, your
own mother, sweet one, your dear mother who loves
you so, and must leave you now and see you no
more!"

Now what it was in that wild plea that touched
the consciousness of the child at last, only God
Himself can say. But first Naomi's cheeks grew
pale at the embrace of the arms that held her, and

then they reddened, and then her little nervous fingers grasped at Ruth's hands again, and then her little lips trembled, and then, at length, she flung herself along Ruth's bosom and nestled close in her embrace.

Ruth fell back on her pillow now with a cry of joy; the black woman stood and wept by the wall; and Israel, unable to bear up his heart any longer, was melted and unmanned. The sun had gone down, and the room was darkening rapidly, for the twilight in that land is short; the streets were quiet, and the mooddin of the neighbouring minaret was chanting in the silence, "God is great, God is great!"

After awhile the little one fell asleep at her mother's bosom, and, seeing this, Fatimah would have lifted her away and carried her back to her own bed; but Ruth said, "No; leave her, let me have her with me while I may."

"No one shall take her from you," said Israel.

Then she gazed down at the child's face and said,

"It is hard to leave her and never once to have heard her voice."

"That is the bitterest cup of all," said Israel.

"I shall not return to her," said Ruth, "but she shall come to me, and then, perhaps—who knows? —perhaps in the resurrection I shall hear it."

Israel made no answer.

Ruth gazed down at the child again, and said, "My helpless darling! Who will care for you when I am gone?"

"Rest, rest, and sleep!" said Israel.

"Ah! yes, I know," said Ruth. "How foolish of me! You are her father, and you love her also. Yet promise me—promise——"

"For love and tending she shall never lack," said Israel. "And now lie you still, my dearest, lie still and sleep."

She stretched out her hand to him. "Yes, that was what I meant," she said, and smiled. Then a shadow crossed her face in the gloom. "But when I am gone," she said, "will Naomi ever know that her mother who is dead had wronged her?"

"You have never wronged her," said Israel. "Have done, oh, have done!"

"God punished us for our prayer, my husband," said Ruth.

"Peace, peace!" said Israel.

"But God is good," said Ruth, "and surely He will not afflict our child much longer."

"Hush! Hush! You will awaken her," said Israel, not thinking what he said. "Now lie-still and sleep, dearest. You are tired also."

She lay quiet for a time, gazing, while the light remained, into the face of the sleeping child, and listening, when the light failed, to her gentle breathing. Then she babbled and crooned over her with a childish joy. "Yes, yes, father is right, and mother must lie quiet—very quiet, and so her little Naomi will sleep long—very long, and wake happy and well in the morning. How bonny she will look! How fresh and rosy!"

She paused a moment. Her laboured breathing came quick and fast. "But shall *I* be here to see her? Shall I?"

She paused again, and then, as though to banish thought, she began to sing in a low voice that was like a moan. Presently her singing ceased, and she spoke again, but this time in broken whispers.

"How soft and glossy her hair is! I wonder if Fatimah will remember to wash it every day. She should twist it around her fingers to keep it in pretty curls. . . . . Oh, why did God make my child so beautiful? . . . . Dear me, her morning frock wanted stitching at the sleeves; it's a chance if Habeebah has seen to it. Then there's her underclothing. . . . . Will she be deaf and blind and dumb always? I wonder if I shall see her when I . . . . They say that angels are sent. . . . . Yes, yes, that's it; when I am there—there—I will go to God and say, 'O Lord! my little girl whom I have left behind, she is . . . . You would never think, O Lord, how many things may happen to one like her. Let me go—only let me watch over—O Lord, let me be her guar—— ' "

Her weakness had conquered her, and she was quiet at last. Israel sat in silence by the post of the bed. His heart was surging itself out of his choking breast. The black woman stood somewhere by the wall. After a time Ruth seemed to awake as from sleep. She was in great excitement.

"Israel, Israel!" she cried in a voice of joy, "I have seen a vision. It was Naomi. She was no longer deaf and blind and dumb. She was grown to be a woman, but I knew her instantly. Not a woman either, but a young maiden, and so beautiful, so beautiful! Yes, and she could see and hear and speak."

Israel thought Ruth had become delirious, and he tried to soothe her, but her agitation was not to be overcome. "The Lord has seen our tears at last," she cried. "He has put our sin beneath His feet. We are forgiven. It will be well with the child yet."

Israel did not try to gainsay her, and at sight and sound of her joy, seeing it so beautiful, yet thinking it so vain, he could not help at last but weep. Presently she became quiet again, and then again, after a little while, she woke as from a sleep.

"I am ready now," she said in a whisper, "quite ready, sweet Heaven, quite, quite ready now."

Then with her one free hand she felt in the darkness for Israel, where he sat beside her, and touching his forehead she smoothed it, and said very softly, "Farewell, my husband!"

And Israel answered her, "Farewell!"

"Good-night!" she whispered.

And Israel drew down her hand from his forehead to his lips and sobbed and said, "Good-night, beloved!"

Then she put her white lips to the child's blind eyes, and at that moment the spirit of the Lord came to her, and the Lord took her, and she died.

When lamps had been brought into the room, and Fatimah saw that the end had come, she would have lifted Naomi from Ruth's bosom, but the child awoke as she was being moved, and clasped her little fingers about the dead mother's neck, and covered the mouth with kisses. And when she felt that the lips did not answer to her lips, and that the arms which had held her did not hold her any longer, but fell away useless she clung the closer, and bright tears started to her eyes.

And Israel groaned in his spirit, and said, "O heavy hour! O vain hope in death! Dost thou not see her now, O Ruth, and where thou art canst thou not wipe away the tears of thy child, and whisper tidings to her soul how she shall meet thee yet again?"

CHAPTER V.

THE people of Tetuan were not melted towards Israel by the depth of his sorrow, and the breadth of shadow that lay upon him. By noon of the day following the night of Ruth's death, Israel knew that he was to be left alone. It was a rule of the Mellah that on notice being given of a death in their quarter the clerk of the synagogue should publish it at the first service thereafter, in order that a body of men, called the Hebra Kadisha of Kabranim, the Holy Society of the Buriers, might straightway make arrangements for burial. Early prayers had been held in the synagogue at eight o'clock that morning, and no one had yet come near to Israel's house. The men of the Hebra were going about their ordinary occupations. They knew nothing of Ruth's death by official announcement. The clerk had not published it. Israel remembered with bitterness that notice of it had not been sent. Nevertheless, the fact was known throughout Tetuan. There was not a water-carrier in the market-place but had taken it to each house he called at, and passed it to every man he met. Little groups of idle Jewish women had been many hours congregated in the streets outside, talking of it in whispers and looking up at the darkened windows with awe. But the synagogue knew nothing of it. Israel had omitted the customary ceremony, and in that omission lay the advantage of his enemies. He must humble himself and send to them. Until he did so they would leave him alone.

Israel did not send. Never once since the birth of Naomi had he crossed the threshold of the synagogue. He would not cross it now, whether in body or in spirit. But he was still a Jew, with Jewish customs, if he had lost the Jewish faith, and it was one of the customs of the Jews that a body should be buried within twenty-four hours, at farthest, from the time of death. He must do something immediately. Some help must be summoned. What help could it be?

It was useless to think of the Muselmeen. No believer would lend a hand to dig a grave for an unbeliever, or to make apparel for his dead. It was just as idle to think of the Jews. If the synagogue knew nothing of this burial, no Jew in the Mellah would be found so poor that he would have need to know more. And of Christians, of any sort or condition, there were none in all Tetuan.

The gall of Israel's heart rose to his throat. Was he to be left alone with his dead wife? Did his enemies wish to see him howk out her grave with his own hands? Or did they expect him to come to them with bowed forehead and bended knee? Either way their reckoning was a mistake. They might leave him terribly and awfully alone—alone in his hour of mourning even as they had left him alone in his hour of rejoicing, when he had married the dear soul who was dead. But his strength and energy they should

not crush : his vital and intellectual force they should
not wither away.   Only one thing they could do to
touch him—they could shrivel up his last impulse of
sweet human sympathy.   They were doing it now.

When Israel had put matters to himself so, he
despatched a message to the Governor at the
Kasbah, and received, in answer, six State prisoners,
fettered in pairs, under the guard of two soldiers.

The burial took place within the limit of twenty-
four hours prescribed by Jewish custom.   It was
twilight when the body was brought down from the
upper room to the patio.   There stood the coffin on
a trestle that had been raised for it on chairs standing back to back.   And there, too, sat Israel, with
Naomi and little black Ali beside him.

Israel's manner was composed ; his face was as firm
as a rock, and his dress was more costly than Tetuan
had ever seen him wear before.   Everything that
related to the burial he had managed himself, down
to the least or poorest detail.   But there was nothing
poor about it in the larger sense.   Israel was a rich

man now, and he set no value on his riches except to subdue the fate that had first beaten him down, and to abash the enemies who still menaced him. Nothing was lacking that money could buy in Tetuan to make this burial an imposing ceremony. Only one thing it wanted—it wanted mourners, and it had but one.

Unlike her father, little Naomi was visibly excited. She ran to and fro, clutched at Israel's clothes and seemed to look into his face, clasped the hand of little Ali and held it long as if in fear. Whether she knew what work was afoot, and, if she knew it, by what channel of soul or sense she learnt it, no man can say. That she was conscious of the presence of many strangers is certain, and when the men from the Kasbah brought the roll of white linen down the stairway, with the two black women clinging to it, kissing its fringe and wailing over it, she broke away from Israel and rushed in among them with a startled cry, and her little white arms upraised. But, whatever her impulse, there was no need to check her.

The moment she had touched the cold body of her mother she crept back in dread to her father's side.

It was a strange procession which then passed out of the patio. Four of the prisoners carried the coffin on their shoulders, walking in pairs according to their fetters. They were gaunt and bony creatures. Hunger had wasted their sallow cheeks, and the air of noisome dungeons had sunken their rheumy eyes. Their clothes were soiled rags, and over them, and concealing them down to their waists and yet lower, hung the deep, rich, velvet pall, with its long silk fringes. In front walked the two remaining prisoners, each bearing a great plume in his left hand—the right arm, as well as the right leg, being chained. On either side was a soldier, carrying a lighted lantern, which burnt small and feeble in the twilight, and last of all came Israel himself, unsupported and alone. Thus they passed through the little crowd of idlers that had congregated at the door, through the streets of the Mellah, and out into the market-place, and up the narrow lane that leads to the chief town gate.

There is something in the very nature of power that demands homage, and the people of Tetuan could not deny it to Israel. As the procession went through the town they cleared a way for it, and they were silent until it had gone. Within the gate of the Mellah, a shochet was killing fowls and taking his tribute of copper coins, but he stopped his work and fell back as the procession approached. A blind beggar crouching at the other side of the gate was reciting passages of the Koran, and two Arabs close at his elbow were wrangling over a game at draughts which they were playing by the light of a flare, but both curses and Koran ceased as the procession passed under the arch. In the market-place a Soosi juggler was performing before a throng of laughing people, and a story-teller was shrieking to the twang of his ginbri; but the audience of the juggler broke up as the procession appeared, and the ginbri of the story-teller was no more heard. The hammering in

the shops of the gun-smiths was stopped, and the
tinkling of the bells of the water-carriers was silenced.
Mules bringing wood from the country were dragged
out of the path, and the town asses, with their
panniers full of street-filth, were drawn up by the
wall. From the market-place and out of the shops,
out of the houses and out of the mosque itself, the
people came trooping in crowds, and they made a
long close line on either side of the course which the
procession must take. And through this avenue of
onlookers the strange company made its way—the
two prisoners bearing the plumes, the four others
bearing the coffin, the two soldiers carrying the
lanterns, and Israel last of all, unsupported and
alone. Nothing was heard in the silence of the
people but the tramp of the feet of the six
men, and the clank of their chains. The light of
the lanterns was on the faces of some of them, and
every one knew them for what they were. It was
on the face of Israel also, yet he did not flinch.
His head was held steadily upward; he looked

neither to the right nor to the left, but strode firmly
along.

The Jewish cemetery was outside the town walls,
and before the procession came to it the darkness had
closed in. Its flat white tombstones, all pointing
towards Jerusalem, lay in the gloom like a flock of
sheep asleep among the grass. It had no gate but a
gap in the fence, and no fence but a hedge of the
prickly pear and the aloe.

Israel had opened a grave for Ruth beside the
grave of the old rabbi her father. He had asked no
man's permission to do so, but, if no one had helped
at that day's business, neither had any one dared to
hinder. And when the coffin was set down by the
grave-side no ceremony did Israel forget, and none
did he omit. He repeated the Kaddesh and cut the
notch in his kaftan; he took from his breast the little
linen bag of the white earth of the land of promise
and laid it under the head; he locked a padlock
and flung away the key. Last of all, when the
body had been taken out of the coffin and lowered

to its long home, he stepped in after it, and called on one of the soldiers to lend him a lantern. And then, kneeling at the foot of his dead wife, he touched her with both his hands, and spoke these words in a clear, firm voice, looking down at her where she lay in the veil that she had used to wear in the synagogue, and speaking to her as though she heard: "Ruth, my wife, my dearest, for the cruel wrong which I did you long ago when I suffered you to marry me, being a man such as I was, under the ban of my people, forgive me now, my beloved, and ask God to forgive me also."

It was a strange sight and a strange sound : the dark cemetery, the six prisoners in their clanking irons, the two soldiers with their lanterns, the open grave, and this strong-hearted man kneeling within it, that he might do his last duty, according to the custom of his race and faith, to her whom he had wronged and should meet no more until the resurrection itself reunited them. The traffic of the streets had begun again by this time, and between the words which Israel had spoken the low hum of many voices had come over the dark town walls.

The six prisoners went back to the Kasbah with joyful hearts, for each carried with him a paper which procured his freedom on the day following. But Israel returned to his home with a soured and darkened mind. As he had plucked his last handful of the grass, and flung it over his shoulder, saying, "They shall spring in the cities as the grass in the earth," he had asked himself what it mattered to him, though all the world were peopled, now that she, who had been all the world to him, was dead. God had left him as a lonely pilgrim in a dreary desert. Only one glimpse of human affection had he known as a man, and here it was taken from him for ever.

And when he remembered Naomi, he quarrelled with God again. She was a helpless exile among men, a creature banished from all human intercourse, a living soul locked in a tabernacle of flesh. Was it a good God who had taken the mother from such a child—the child from such a mother? Israel was heart-smitten, and his soul blasphemed. It was not God but the devil that ruled the world. It was not justice but evil that governed it.

Thus did this outcast man rebel against God, thinking of the child's loss and of his own; but nevertheless by the child itself he was yet to be saved from the devil's snare, and the ways wherein this sweet flower, fresh from God's hand, wrought upon his heart to redeem it were very strange and beautiful.

CHAPTER VI

OF THE SPIRIT-MAID.

THE promise which Israel made to Ruth at her death that Naomi should not lack for love and tending he faithfully fulfilled. From that time forward he became as father and mother both to the child.

At the outset of his charge he made a survey of her condition, and found it more terrible than imagination of the mind could think or words of the tongue express. It was easy to say that she was deaf and dumb and blind, but it was hard to realise what so great an affliction implied. It implied that she was a little human sister standing close to the rest of the family of man, yet very far away from them. She was as much apart as if she had inhabited a different sphere. No human sympathy could reach her in joy or pain and sorrow. She had no part to

play in life. In the midst of a world of light she
was in a land of darkness, and she was in a world of
silence in the midst of a land of sweet sounds. She
was a living and buried soul.

And of that soul itself, what did Israel know?
He knew that it had memory, for Naomi had remembered her mother; and he knew that it had love, for
she had pined for Ruth, and clung to her. But what
were love and memory without sight and speech?
They were no more than a magnet locked in a casket
—idle and useless to any purposes of man or the
world.

Thinking of this, Israel realised for the first time
how awful was the affliction of his motherless girl.
To be blind was to be afflicted once, but to be both
blind and deaf was not only to be afflicted twice, but
twice ten thousand times, and to be blind and deaf
and dumb was not merely to be afflicted thrice, but
beyond all reckonings of human speech.

For though Naomi had been blind, yet, if she could
have had hearing, her father might have spoken with

her, and if she had sorrows he must have soothed them, and if she had joys he must have shared them, and in this beautiful world of God, so full of things to look upon and to love, he must have been eyes of her eyes that could not see. On the other hand, though Naomi had been deaf, yet if she could have had sight her father might have held intercourse with her by the light of her eyes, and if she felt pain he must have seen it, and if she had found pleasure he must have known it, and what man is, and what woman is, and what the world and what the sea and what the sky, would have been as an open book for her to read. But, being blind and deaf together, and, by fault of being deaf, being dumb as well, what word was to describe the desolation of her state, the blank void of her isolation--cut off, apart, aloof, shut in, imprisoned, enchained, a soul without communion with other souls: alive, and yet dead?

Thus realising Naomi's condition in the deep infirmity of her nature, Israel set himself to consider how he could reach her darkened and silent soul. And first he tried to learn what good gifts were left to her that he might foster them to her advantage and nourish them to his own great comfort and joy. Yet no gift whatever could he find in her but the one gift only whereof he had known from the beginning—the gift of touch and feeling. With this he must make her to see, or else her light should always be darkness, and with this he must make her to hear, or silence should be her speech for ever.

Then he remembered that during his years in England he had heard strange stories of how the dumb had been made to speak though they could not hear, and the blind and deaf to understand and to answer. So he sent to England for many books, written on the treatment of these children of affliction, and when they were come he pondered them closely and was thrilled by the marvellous works they described. But when he came to practise the precepts they had given him, his spirits flagged, for the impediments were great. Time after time he tried, and failed always, to touch by so much as one shaft of

light the hidden soul of the child through its tene-
ment of flesh and blood. Neither the simplest
thought nor the poorest element of an idea found any
way to her mind, so dense were the walls of the prison
that encompassed it. " Yes " was a mystery that
could not at first be revealed to her, and " No " was
a problem beyond her power to apprehend. Smiles
and frowns were useless to teach her. No discipline
could be addressed to her mind or heart. Except
mere bodily restraint, no control could be imposed
upon her. She was swayed by her impulses alone.

Israel did not despair. If he was broken down
to-day he strengthened his hands for to-morrow. At
length he had got so far, after a world of toil and
thought, that Naomi knew when he patted her head
that it was for approval, and when he touched her
hand it was for assent. Then he stopped very
suddenly. His hope had not drooped, and neither
had his energy failed, but the conviction had fastened
upon him that such effort in his case must be an
offence against Heaven. Naomi was not merely an

infirm creature from the left hand of Nature; she was an afflicted being from the right hand of God. She was a living monument of sin that was not her own. It was useless to go farther. The child must be left where God had placed her.

But meanwhile, if Naomi lacked the senses of the rest of the human kind, she seemed to communicate with Nature by other organs than they possessed. It was as if the spiritual world itself must have taught her, and from that source alone could she have imbibed her power. To tell of all she could do to guide her steps, and to minister to her pleasures, and to cherish her affections, would be to go beyond the limit of belief. Truly it seemed as if Naomi, being blind with her bodily eyes, could yet look upon a light that no one else could see, and, being deaf with her bodily ears, could yet listen to voices that no one else could hear.

Thus, if she came skipping through the corridor of the patio, she knew when any one approached her, for she would hold out her hands and stop. Nay;

but she knew also who it would be as well as if her
eyes or ears had taught her; for always, if it was her
father, she reached out her hands to take his left
hand in both of hers, and then she pressed it against
her cheek; and always, if it was little Ali, she curved
her arms to encircle his neck; and always, if it was
Fatimah, she leapt up to her bosom; and always, if it
was Habeebah, she passed her by. Did she go with
Ali into the streets, she knew the Mellah gate from
the gate of the town, and the narrow lanes from the
open Sôk. Did she pass the lofty mosque in the
market-place, she knew it from the low shops that
nestled under and behind and around. Did a troop
of mules and camels come near her, she knew them
from a crowd of people; and did she pass where two
streets crossed, she would stand and face both ways.

And as the years grew she came to know all places
within and around Tetuan, the town of the Moors
and the Mellah of the Jews, the Kasbah and the
narrow lane leading up to it, the fort on the hill and
the river under the town walls, the mountains on

either side of the valley, and even some of their rocky gorges. She could find her way among them all without help or guidance, and no control could any one impose upon her to keep her out of the way of harm. While Ali was a little fellow he was her constant companion, always ready for any adventure that her unquiet heart suggested; but when he grew to be a boy, and was sent to school every day early and late, she would fare forth alone save for a tiny white goat which her father had bought to be another playfellow.

And because feeling was sight to her, and touch was hearing, and the crown of her head felt the winds of the heavens and the soles of her feet felt the grass of the fields, she loved best to go bareheaded whether the sun was high or the air was cool, and barefooted also, from the rising of the morning until the coming of the stars. So, casting off her slippers and the great straw hat which a Jewish maiden wears, and clad in her white woollen shawl, wrapped loosely about her in folds of airy grace, and with the little goat going before her, though she saw it not, and neither heard its bleat nor the beat of its feet, she would climb the hill beyond the battery, even to the topmost peak of it, and stand on the summit, like a spirit poised in air. Nothing could she see of the green valley then stretched before her, or of the white town lying below, with its domes and minarets, but she seemed to exult in her lofty place, and to drink new life from the rush of mighty winds about her. Then coming back to the dale, she would seem, to those who looked up at her, with fear and with awe, to leap as the goat leapt in the rocky places; and as a bird sweeps over the grass with wings outstretched, so with her arms spread out, and her long fair hair flying loose, she would seem to sweep down the hill, as though her very tiptoes did not touch it.

By what power she did these things no man could tell, except it were the power of the spiritual world itself; but the distemper of the mind, which loved such dangers, increased upon her as she grew

from a child into a maid, and it found new ways of
strangeness. Thus, in the spring, when the rain fell
heavily, or in the winter, when the great winds were
abroad, or in the summer, when the lightning
lightened and the thunder thundered, her restless
spirit seemed to be roused to sympathetic tumults,
and if she could escape the eyes that watched her she
would run and race in the tempest, and her eyes
would be aglitter, and laughter would be on her lips.
Then Israel himself would go out to find her, and,
having found her in the pelting storm without cover-
ing on her head or shoes on her feet, he would fetch
her home by the hand, and as they passed through
the streets together his forehead would be bowed and
his eyes bent down.

But it was not always that Naomi made her father
ashamed. More often her joyful spirit cheered him,
for above all things else she was a creature of joy.
A circle of joy seemed to surround her always. Her
heart in its darkness was full of radiance. As she grew
her comeliness increased, though this was strange and

touching in her beauty, that her face did not become older with her years, but was still the face of a child, with a child's expression of sweetness through the bloom and flush of early maidenhood. Her love of flowers increased also, and the sense of smell seemed to come to her, for she filled the house with all fragrant flowers in their season, twining them in wreaths about the white pillars of the patio, and binding them in rings around the brown water-jars that stood in it. And with the girl's expanding nature her love of dress increased as well; but it was not a young maid's love of lovely things; it was a wild passion for light, loose garments that swayed and swirled in native grace about her. Truly she was a spirit of joy and gladness. She was happy as a day in summer, and fresh as a dewy morning in spring. The ripple of her laughter was like sunshine. A flood of sunshine seemed to follow in the air wheresoever she went. And certainly for Israel, her father, she was as a sunbeam gathering sunshine into his lonely house.

Nevertheless, the sunbeam had its cloud-shapes of gloom, and if Israel in his darker hours hungered for more human company, and wished that the little playfellow of the angels which had come down to his dwelling could only be his simple human child, he sometimes had his wish, and many throbs of anguish with it. For often it happened, and especially at seasons when no winds were stirring, and blank peace and a doleful silence haunted the air, that Naomi would seem to fall into a sick longing from causes that were beyond Israel's power to fathom. Then her sweet face would sadden, and her beautiful blind eyes would fill, and her pretty laughter would echo no more through the house. And sometimes, in the dead of the night, she would rise from her bed and go through the dark corridors, for darkness and light were as one to her, until she came to Israel's room, and he would awake from his sleep to find her, like a little white vision, standing by his bedside. What she wanted there he could never know, for neither had he power to ask nor she to answer, whether she were sick or in pain, or whether in her sleep she had seen a face from the invisible world, and heard a voice that called her away, or whether her mother's arms had seemed to be about her once again and then to be torn from her afresh, and she had come to him on awakening in her trouble, not knowing what it is to dream, but thinking all evil dreams to be true fact and new sorrow. So, with a sigh, he would arise and light his lamp and lead her back to her bed, and more scalding than the tears that would be standing in Naomi's eyes would be the hot drops that would gush into his own.

Most of all when such things befell would Israel long for some miracle out of heaven to find a way to the little maiden's mind that she might ask and answer and know, yet he dared not to pray for it, for still greater than his pity for the child was his fear of the wrath of God. And out of this fear there came to him at length an awful and terrible thought: though so severed on earth, his child and he, yet before the bar of judgment they would one day be brought together, and then how should it stand with her soul?

Naomi knew nothing of God, having no way of speech with man. Would God condemn her for that, and cast her out for ever? No, no, no! God would not ask her for good works in the land of silence, and for labour in the land of night. She had no eyes to see God's beautiful world, and no ears to hear His holy word. God had created her so, and He would not destroy what He had made. Far rather would He look with love and pity on His little one, so long and sorely tried on earth, and send her at last to be a blessed saint in heaven.

Israel tried to comfort himself so, but the effort was vain. He was a Jew to the inmost fibre of his being, and he answered himself out of his own mouth that it was his own sinful wish, and not God's will, that had sent Naomi into the world as she was. Then, on the day of the great account, how should he answer to her for her soul?

Visions stood up before him of endless retribution
for the soul that knew not God. These were the
most awful terrors of his sleepless nights, but at
length peace came to him, for he saw his path of
duty. It was his duty to Naomi that he should tell
her of God and reveal the word of the Lord to her!
What matter if she could not hear? Though she
had senses as the sands of the seashore, yet in the
way of light the Lord alone could lead her. What
matter though she could not see? The soul was the
eye that saw God, and with bodily eyes had no man
seen Him.

So every day thereafter at sunset Israel took
Naomi by the hand and led her to an upper room, the
same wherein her mother died, and, fetching from a
cupboard of the wall the Book of the Law, he read
to her of the commandments of the Lord by Moses,
and of the Prophets, and of the Kings. And while
he read, Naomi sat in silence at his feet, with his
one free hand in both of her hands, clasped close
against her cheek.

What the little maid in her darkness thought of this custom, what mystery it was to her and wherefore, only the eye that looks into darkness could see; but it was so at length that as soon as the sun had set—for she knew when the sun was gone—Naomi herself would take her father by the hand, and lead him to the upper room, and fetch the book to his knees.

And sometimes as Israel read, an evil spirit would seem to come to him, and make a mock at him, and say, "The child is deaf and hears not—go read your book in the tombs!" But he only hardened his neck and laughed proudly. And, again, sometimes the evil spirit seemed to say, "Why waste yourself in this misspent desire? The child is buried while she is still alive, and who shall roll away the stone?" But Israel only answered, "It is for the Lord to do miracles, and the Lord is mighty."

So, great in his faith, Israel read to Naomi night after night, and when his spirit was sore of many taunts in the day his voice would be hoarse, and he would read the law which says, " *Thou shalt not curse the deaf, nor put a stumbling-block before the blind.*" But when his heart was at peace his voice would be soft, and he would read of the child Samuel sanctified to the Lord in the temple, and how the Lord called him and he answered—

" *And it came to pass at that time, when Eli was laid down in his place, and his eyes began to wax dim that he could not see ; and ere the lamp of God went out, in the temple of the Lord, where the Ark of God was, and Samuel was laid down to sleep, that the Lord called Samuel, and he answered, Here am I. And he ran unto Eli and said, Here am I, for thou callest me. And he said, I called not ; lie down again. And he went and lay down. And the Lord called yet again, Samuel. And Samuel rose and went to Eli and said, Here am I, for thou didst call me. And he answered, I called not, my son ; lie down again. Now Samuel did not yet know the Lord, neither was the Word of the Lord yet revealed to him.*"

And, having finished his reading, Israel would close

the book and sing out of the Psalms of David the psalm which says: "It is good for me that I have been in trouble, that I may learn Thy statutes."

Thus, night after night, when the sun was gone down, did Israel read of the law and sing of the Psalms to Naomi, his daughter, who was both blind and deaf. And though Naomi heard not, and neither did she see, yet in their silent hour together there was another in their chamber always with them—there was a third, for there was God.

CHAPTER VII.

OF THE ANGEL IN ISRAEL'S HOUSE.

WHEN Israel had been some twenty years at Tetuan, Naomi being then fourteen years of age, Ben Aboo, the Basha, married a Christian wife. The woman's name was Katrina. She was a Spaniard by birth, and had first come to Morocco at the tail of a Spanish embassy, which travelled through Tetuan from Ceuta to the Sultan at Fez. What her belongings were, and what her antecedents had been, no one appeared to know, nor did Ben Aboo himself seem to care. She answered all his present needs in her own person, which was ample in its proportions and abundant in its charms.

In marrying Ben Aboo, the wily Katrina imposed two conditions. The first was that he should put away the full Mohammedan complement of four

Moorish wives, whom he had married already, as well as the many concubines that he had annexed in his way through life, and now kept lodged in one unquiet nest in the women's hidden quarter of the Palace. The second condition was that she herself should never be banished to such seclusion, but, like the wife of any European governor, should openly share the state of her husband.

Ben Aboo was in no mood to stand on the rights of a strict Mohammedan, and he accepted both of her conditions. The first he never meant to abide by, but the second she took care he should observe, and, as a prelude to that public life which she intended to live by his side, she insisted on a public marriage.

They were married according to the rites of the Catholic Church by a Franciscan friar settled at Tangier, and the marriage festival lasted six days. Great was the display, and lavish the outlay. Every morning the cannon of the fort fired a round of shot from the hill, every evening the tribesmen from the mountains went through their feats of powder-play in the market-place, and every night a body of Aïssáwà from Mequinez yelled and shrieked in the enclosure called the M'salla, near the Bab er-Remoosh. Feasts were spread in the Kasbah, and relays of guests from among the chief men of the town were invited daily to partake of them.

No man dared to refuse his invitation, or to neglect the tribute of a present, though the Moors well knew that they were lending the light of their countenance to a brazen outrage on their faith, and though it galled the hearts of the Jews to make merry at the marriage of a Christian and a Muslim—no man except Israel, and he excused himself with what grace he could, being in no mood for rejoicing, but sick with sorrow of the heart.

The Spanish woman was not to be gainsaid. She had taken her measure of the man, and had resolved that a servant so powerful as Israel should pay her court and tribute before all. Therefore she caused him to be invited again; but Israel had taken his measure of the woman, and with some lack of courtesy he excused himself afresh.

Katrina was not yet done. She was a creature of resource, and having heard of Naomi, with strange stories concerning her, she devised a children's feast for the last day of the marriage festival, and caused Ben Aboo to write to Israel a formal letter, beginning, " To our well-beloved the excellent Israel ben Oliel, Praise to the one God," and setting forth that on the morrow, when the " Sun of the world " should " place his foot in the stirrup of speed," and gallop " from the kingdom of shades," the Governor would " hold a gathering of delight " for all the children of Tetuan, and he, Israel, was besought to " lighten it with the rays of his face, rivalled only by the sun," and to bring with him his little daughter Naomi, whose arrival, " similar to a spring breeze," should " dissipate the dark night of solitude and isolation." This despatch, written in the common cant of the people, concluded with quotations from the Prophet on brotherly love, and a significant and more sincere

assurance that the Basha would not admit of excuses
" of the thickness of a hair."

When Israel received the missive, his anger was
hot and furious.   He leapt to the conclusion that, in
demanding the presence of Naomi, the Spanish
woman, who must know of the child's condition,
desired only to make a show of it.   But, after a
time, he put that thought from him as uncharitable
and unwarranted, and resolved to obey the
summons.

And, indeed, if he had felt any further diffi-
dence, the sight of Naomi's own eagerness must
have driven it away.   The little maid seemed to
know that something unusual was going on.
Troops of poor villagers from every miserable
quarter of the bashalic came into the town each
day, beating drums, firing long guns, driving their
presents before them—bullocks, cows, and sheep—
and trying to make believe that they rejoiced and
were glad.   Naomi appeared to be conscious of
many tents pitched in the market-place, of denser

crowds in the streets, and of much bustle everywhere.

Also she seemed to catch the contagion of little Ali's excitement. The children of all the schools of the town, both Jewish and Moorish, had been summoned through their Tálebs to the festival; there was to be dancing and singing and playing on musical instruments; and Ali himself, who had lately practised the kánoon—the lute, the harp—under his teacher, was to show his skill before the Governor. Therefore, great was the little black man's excitement, and, in the fever of it, he would talk to every one of the event forthcoming—to Fatimah, to Habeebah, and often to Naomi also, until the memory of her infirmity would come to him, or perhaps the derisive laugh of his schoolfellows would stop him, and then, thinking they were laughing at the girl, he would fall on them like a fury, and they would scamper away.

When the great day came, Ali went off to the Kasbah with his school and Táleb, in the long pro-

cession of many schools and many Tálebs.   It was a
strange and touching spectacle, whereat a man's eyes
might fill and his gorge rise together.   Every child
carried a present for the rich Basha; now a boy with
a goat, then a girl with a lamb, again a poor tattered
mite with a hen, all cuddling them close like pets
they must part with, yet all looking radiantly happy
in their sweet innocency, which had no alloy of pain
from the tree of the knowledge of good and evil.

Israel took Naomi by the hand, but no present
with either of them, and followed the children, going
past the booths, the blind beggars, the lepers, and
the shrieking Arabs that lay thick about the gate,
through the iron-clamped door, and into the quad-
rangle, where groups of women stood together closely
covered in their blankets—the mothers and sisters of
the children, permitted to see their little ones pass
into the Kasbah, but allowed to go no farther—then
down the crooked passage, past the tiny mosque, like
a closet, and the bath, like a dungeon, and finally
into the pillared patio, paved and walled with tiles.

This was the place of the festival, and it was filled already with a great company of children, their fathers and their teachers. Moors, Arabs, Berbers, and Jews, clad in their various costumes of white and blue and black and red—they were a gorgeous, a voluptuous, and, perhaps, a beautiful spectacle in the morning sunlight.

As Israel entered, with Naomi by the hand, he was conscious that every eye was on them, and as they passed through the way that was made for them, he heard the whispered exclamations of the people. "Shoof!" muttered a Moor. "See!" "It's himself," said a Jew. "And the child," said another Jew. "Allah has smitten her," said an Arab. "Blind and dumb and deaf," said another Moor. "God be gracious to my father!" said another Arab.

Musicians were playing in the gallery that ran round the court, and from the flat roof above it the women of the Governor's hareem, not yet dispersed, his four lawful Mohammedan wives, and many concubines, were gazing furtively down from behind their haiks.   There was a fountain in the middle of the patio, and at the farther end of it, within an alcove that opened out of a horseshoe arch, beneath ceilings hung with stalactites, against walls covered with silken haities, and on Rabat rugs of many colours, sat Ben Aboo and his Christian bride.

It was there that Israel saw the Spaniard for the first time, and at the instant of recognition he shivered as with cold.   She was a handsome woman, but plainly a heartless one—selfish, vain, and vulgar.

Ben Aboo hailed Israel with welcomes and peace-blessings, and Katrina drew Naomi to her side.

"So this is the little maid of whom wonderful rumours are so rife ?" said Katrina.

Israel bent his head and shuddered at seeing the child at the woman's feet.

"The darling is as fair as an angel," said Katrina, and she kissed Naomi.

The kiss seemed to Israel to smite his own cheeks like a blow.

Then the performances of the children began, and

truly they made a pretty and affecting sight; the white walls, the deep blue sky, the black shadows of the gallery, the bright sunlight, the grown people massed around the patio, and these sweet little faces coming and going in the middle of it. First, a line of Moorish girls in their embroidered hazzams dancing after their native fashion, bending and rising, twisting and turning, but keeping their feet in the same place constantly. Then, a line of Jewish girls in their kilted skirts dancing after the Jewish manner, tripping on their slippered toes, whirling and turning around with rapid motions, and playing timbrels and tambourines held high above their heads by their shapely arms and hands. Then passages of the Koran chanted by a group of Moorish boys in their jellabs, purple and chocolate and white, peaked above their red tarbooshes. Then a psalm by a company of Jewish boys in their black skull-caps—a brave old song of Zion sung by silvery young voices in an alien land. Finally, little black Ali, led out by his teacher, with his diminutive Moorish harp in his hands, showing

no fear at all, but only a negro boy's shy looks of
pleasure—his head aside, his eyes gleaming, his white
teeth glinting, and his face aglow.

Now down to this moment Naomi, at the feet of
the woman, had been agitated and restless, sometimes
rising, then sinking back, sometimes playing with
her nervous fingers, and then pushing off her slippers.
It was as though she was conscious of the fine show
which was going forward, and knew that they were
children who were making it.   Perhaps the breath of
the little ones beat her on the level of her cheeks, or
perhaps the light air made by the sweep of their
garments was wafted to her sensitive body.   Whatsoever the sense whereby the knowledge came to her,
clearly it was there in her flushed and twitching face,
which was full of that old hunger for child-company
which Israel knew too well.

But when little Ali was brought out and he began
to play on his kánoon, his harp, it was impossible to
repress Naomi's excitement. The girl leaped up from
her place at the woman's feet, and with the utmost

rapidity of motion she passed like a gleam of light across the patio to the boy's side. And, being there, she touched the harp as he played it, and then a low cry came from her lips. Again she touched it, and her eyes, though blind, seemed for an instant to flame like fire. Then, with both her hands she clung to it, and with her lips and her tongue she kissed it, while her whole body quivered like a reed in the wind.

Israel saw what she did, and his very soul trembled at the sight with wild thoughts that did not dare to take the name of hope. As well as he could in the confusion of his own senses he stepped forward to draw the little maiden back, but the wife of the Governor called on him to leave her.

"Leave her!" she cried. "Let us see what the child will do!"

At that moment Ali's playing came to an end, and the boy let the harp pass to Naomi's clinging fingers, and then, half sitting, half kneeling on the ground beside it, the girl took it to herself. She caressed it, she patted it with her hand, she touched its strings, and then a faint smile crossed her rosy lips. She laid her cheek against it and touched its strings again, and then she laughed aloud. She flung off her slippers and the garment that covered her beautiful arms, and laid her pure flesh against the harp wheresoever her flesh might cling, and touched its strings once more, and then her very heart seemed to laugh with delight.

Now, what is to follow will seem to be no better than a superstitious saying, but true it is, nevertheless, and simple sooth for all it sounds so strange, that though Naomi was deaf as the grave, and had never yet heard music, and though she was untaught and knew nothing of the notes of a harp to strike them, yet she swept the strings to strange harmonies such as no man had ever listened to before and none could follow.

It was not music that the little maiden made to her ear, but only motion to her body, and just as the deaf who are deaf alone are sometimes found to take pleasure in all forms of percussion, and to derive from them some of the sensations of sound—the trembling of the air after thunder, the quivering of the earth after cannon, and the quaking of vast walls after the ringing of mighty bells—so Naomi, who was blind as well and had no sense save touch, found in her fingers, which had gathered up the force of all the other senses, the power to reproduce on this instrument of music the movement of all things that moved about her—the patter of the leaves of the fig-tree in the patio of her home, the swirl of the great winds on the hill-top, the plash of rain on her face, and the rippling of the levanter in her hair.

This was all the witchery of Naomi's playing, yet, because every emotion in Nature has its harmony, so there was harmony of some wild sort in the music that was struck by the girl's fingers out of the strings of the harp.   But, more than her music, which was, perhaps, only a rhapsody of sound, was the frenzy of the girl herself as she made it.   She lifted her head like a bird, her throat swelled, her bosom heaved, and, as she played, she laughed again and again.

There was something fascinating and magical in the spectacle of the beautiful fair face aglow with joy, the rounded limbs (visible through the robes) clinging to the sides of the harp, and the delicate white fingers flying across the strings. There was something gruesome and awful, as well, for the face of the girl was blind, and her ears heard nothing of the music that her fingers were making.

Every eye was on her, and in the wide circle around every mouth was agape. And when those who looked on and listened had recovered from their first surprise, very strange and various were the whispered words they passed between them. "Where has she learnt it?" asked a Moor. "From her master himself," muttered a Jew. "Who is it?" asked the Moor. "Beelzebub," growled the Jew. "God pity me, the evil eye is on her," said an Arab. "God will show," said a Shereef from Wazzán, "They say her mother was a childless woman, and offered petitions for Hannah's blessing at the tomb of Rabbi Amran." "No," said the Arab; "she sent her girdle." "Anyhow, the child is a saint," whispered the Shereef. "No, but a devil," snorted the Jew.

"Brava, brava, brava!" cried the new wife of Ben Aboo, and she cheered and laughed as the girl played. "What did I tell you?" she said, looking toward her husband. "The child is not deaf, no, nor blind either. Oh, it's a brave imposture! Brava, brava!"

Still the little maiden played, but now her brow was clouded, her head dropped, her eyelashes were downcast, and she hung over the harp and sighed audibly.

"Good again!" cried the woman. "Very good!" and she clapped her hands, whereupon the Arabs and the Moors, forgetting their dread, felt constrained to follow her example, and they cheered in their wilder way, but the Jews continued to mutter, "Beelzebub, Beelzebub!"

Israel saw it all, and at first, amid the commotion of his mind and the confusion of his senses, his heart melted at sight of what Naomi did. Had God opened a gateway to her soul? Were the poor wings of her spirit to spread themselves out at last? Was this, then, the way of speech that Heaven had given her? But hardly had Israel overflowed with the tenderness of such thoughts when the bleating and barking of the faces about him awakened his anger. Then, like blows on his brain, came the cries of the wife of the Governor, who cheered this awakening of the girl's soul, as it were no better than a vulgar show; and at that Israel's wrath rose to his throat.

"Brava, brava!" cried the woman again; and, turning to Israel, she said, "You shall leave the child with me. I must have her with me always."

Israel's throat seemed to choke him at that word. He looked at Katrina, and saw that she was a woman lustful of breath and vain of heart, who had married Ben Aboo because he was rich. Then he looked at Naomi, and remembered that her heart was clear as the water, and sweet as the morning, and pure as the snow.

And at that moment the wife of the Governor cheered again, and again the people echoed her, and even the women on the housetops made bold to take up her cry with their cooing ululation. The playing had ceased, the spell had dissolved, Naomi's fingers had fallen from the harp, her head had dropped into her breast, and with a sigh she had sunk forward on to her face.

"Take her in!" said the wife of Ben Aboo, and two Arab soldiers stepped up to where the little maiden lay. But before they had touched her Israel strode out with swollen lips and distended nostrils.

"Stop!" he cried.

The Arabs hesitated, and looked towards their master.

"Do as you are bidden—take her in!" said Ben Aboo.

"Stop!" cried Israel again, in a loud voice that rang through the court. Then, parting the Arabs with a sweep of his arms, he picked up the uncon-

scious maiden, and faced about on the new wife of
Ben Aboo.

"Madam," he cried, "I, Israel ben Oliel, may
belong to the Governor; but my child belongs to
me."

So saying, he passed out of the court, carrying the
girl in his arms, and in the dead silence and blank
stupor of that moment none seemed to know what he
had done until he was gone.

Israel went home in his anger; but, nevertheless,
out of this event he found courage of his heart to
begin of his task again. Let his enemies bleat and
bark "Beelzebub," yet the child was an angel, though
suffering for his sin, and her soul was with God.
She was a spirit, and the songs she had played were
the airs of paradise. But, comforting himself so,
Israel remembered the vision of Ruth, wherein
Naomi had recovered her powers. He had put it
from him hitherto as the delirium of death, but
would the Lord yet bring it to pass? Would God in
His mercy some day take the angel out of his house,

though so strangely gifted, so radiant and beautiful and joyful, and give him instead for the hunger of his heart as a man this sweet human child, his little fair-haired Naomi, though helpless and simple and weak?

CHAPTER VIII.

ISRAEL'S instinct had been sure: the coming of Katrina proved to be the beginning of his end. He kept his office, but he lost his power. No longer did he work his own will in Tetuan; he was required to work the will of the woman. Katrina's will was an evil one, and Israel got the blame of it, for still he seemed to stand in all matters of tribute and taxation between the people and the Governor. It galled him to take the woman's wages, but it vexed him yet more to do her work. Her work was to burden the people with taxes beyond all their power of paying; her wages, was to be hated as the bane of the Bashalic, to be clamoured against as the tyrant of Tetuan, and to be ridiculed by the very offal of the streets.

One day a gang of dirty Arabs in the market-place dressed up a blind beggar in clothes such as Israel wore, and sent him abroad through the town to beg as one that was destitute and in a miserable condition. But nothing seemed to move Israel to pity. Men were cast into prison for no reason save that they were rich, and the relations of such as were there already were allowed to redeem them for money, so that no felon suffered punishment except such as could pay nothing. People took fright and fled to other cities. Israel's name became a curse and a reproach throughout Barbary.

Yet all this time the man's soul was yearning with pity for the people. Since the death of Ruth his heart had grown merciful. The care of the child had softened him. It had brought him to look on other children with tenderness, and looking tenderly on other children had led him to think of other fathers with compassion. Young or old, powerful or weak, mighty or mean, they were all as little children—

helpless children who would sleep together in the same bed soon.

Thinking so, Israel would have undone the evil work of earlier years; but that was impossible now. Many of them that had suffered were dead; some that had been cast into prison had got their last and long discharge. At least Israel would have relaxed the rigour whereby his master ruled, but that was impossible also. Katrina had come, and she was a vain woman and a lover of all luxury, and she commanded Israel to tax the people afresh. He obeyed her through three bad years; but many a time his heart reproached him that he dealt corruptly by the poor people, and when he saw them borrowing money for the Governor's tributes on their lands and houses, and when he stood by while they and their sons were cast into prison for the bonds which they could not pay to the usurers Abraham or Judah or Reuben, then his soul cried out against him that he ate the bread of such a mistress.

But out of the eater came forth meat, and out of

·the strong came forth sweetness, and out of this coming of the Spanish wife of Ben Aboo came deliverance for Israel from the torment of his false position.

Now there was an aged and pious Moor in Tetuan, called Âbd Allah, who was rumoured to have made savings from his business as a gunsmith. Going to mosque one evening, with fifteen dollars in his waistband, he unstrapped his belt and laid it on the edge of the fountain while he washed his feet before entering, for his back was no longer supple. Then a younger Moor, coming to pray at the same time, saw the dollars, and snatched them up and ran. Âbd Allah could not follow the thief, so he went to the Kasbah and told his story to the Governor.

Just at that time Ben Aboo had the Kaid of Fez on a visit to him. "Ask him how much more he has got," whispered the brother Kaid to Ben Aboo.

Âbd Allah answered that he did not know.

"I'll give you two hundred dollars for the chance of all he has," the Kaid whispered again.

"Five bees are better than a pannier of flies—done!" said Ben Aboo.

So Âbd Allah was sold like a sheep and carried to Fez, and there cast into prison on a penalty of two hundred and fifty dollars imposed upon him on the pretence of a false accusation.

Israel sat by the Governor that day at the gate of the hall of justice, and many poor people of the town stood huddled together in the court outside while the evil work was done. No one heard the Kaid of Fez when he whispered to Ben Aboo, but every one saw when Israel drew the warrant that consigned the gunsmith to prison, and when he sealed it with the Governor's seal.

Âbd Allah had made no savings, and, being too old for work, he had lived on the earnings of his son. The son's name was Absalam (Abd es-Salám), and he had a wife whom he loved very tenderly, and one child, a boy of six years of age. Absalam followed his father to Fez, and visited him in prison. The old man had been ordered a hundred lashes, and the flesh was hanging from his limbs. Absalam was great of heart, and, in pity of his father's miserable condition, he went to the Governor and begged that the old man might be liberated, and that he might be imprisoned instead. His petition was heard. Âbd Allah was set free, Absalam was cast into prison, and the penalty was raised from two hundred and fifty dollars to three hundred.

Israel heard of what had happened, and he hastened to Ben Aboo in great agitation, intending to say, "Pay back this man's ransom, in God's name, and his children and his children's children will live to bless you." But when he got to the Kasbah, Katrina was sitting with her husband, and at sight of the woman's face Israel's tongue was frozen.

Absalam had been the favourite of his neighbours among all the gunsmiths of the market-place, and after he had been three months at Fez they made common cause of his calamities, sold their goods at a sacrifice, collected the three hundred dollars of his fine, bought him out of prison, and went in a body through the gate to meet him upon his return to Tetuan. But his wife had died in the meantime, of fear and privation, and only his aged father and his little son were there to welcome him.

"Friends," he said to his neighbours standing outside the walls, "what is the use of sowing if you know not who will reap?"

"No use, no use!" answered several voices.

"If God gives you anything, this man Israel takes it away," said Absalam.

"True, true! Curse him! Curse his relations!" cried the others.

"Then why go back into Tetuan?" said Absalam.

"Tangier is no better," said one. "Fez is worse," said another. "Where is there to go?" said a third.

"Into the plains," said Absalam—"into the plains and into the mountains, for they belong to God alone."

That word was like the flint to the tinder.

"They who have least are richest, and they that have nothing are best off of all," said Absalam, and his neighbours shouted that it was so.

" God will clothe us as he clothes the fields," said Absalam, "and feed our children as he feeds the birds."

In three days' time ten shops in the market-place, on the side of the mosque, were sold up and closed, and the men who had kept them were gone away with their wives and children to live in tents with Absalam on the barren plains beyond the town.

When Israel heard of what had been done he secretly rejoiced; but Ben Aboo was in a commotion of fear, and Katrina was fierce with anger, for the doctrine which Absalam had preached to his neighbours outside the walls was not his own doctrine merely, but that of a great man lately risen among the people, called Mohammed of Mequinez, nicknamed by his enemies Mohammed the Third.

" This madness is spreading," said Ben Aboo.

" Yes," said Katrina; "and if all men follow

where these men lead, who will supply the tables of
Kaids and Sultans?"

"What can I do with them?" said Ben Aboo.

"Eat them up," said Katrina.

Ben Aboo proceeded to put a literal interpretation
upon his wife's counsel. With a company of cavalry
he prepared to follow Absalam and his little fellowship, taking Israel along with him to reckon their
taxes, that he might compel them to return to Tetuan,
and be town-dwellers and house-dwellers, and buy
and sell and pay tribute as before, or else deliver
themselves to prison.

But Absalam and his people had secret word that
the Governor was coming after them, and Israel with
him. So they rolled their tents, and fled to the
mountains that are midway between Tetuan and the
Reef country, and took refuge in the gullies of that
rugged land, living in caves of the rock, with only
the table-land of mountain behind them, and nothing
but a rugged precipice in front. This place they
selected for its safety, intending to push forward, as

occasion offered, to the sanctuaries of Shâwan, trust-
ing rather to the humanity of the wild people, called
the Shâwanis, than to the mercy of their late cruel
masters. But the valley wherein they had hidden is
thick with trees, and Ben Aboo tracked them and came
up with them before they were aware. Then, sending
soldiers to the mountain at the back of the caves,
with instructions that they should come down to the
precipice steadily, and kill none that they could
take alive, Ben Aboo himself drew up at the foot
of it, and Israel with him, and there called on the
people to come out and deliver themselves to his
will.

When the poor people came from their hiding-places
and saw that they were surrounded, and that escape
was not left to them on any side, they thought their
death was sure. But without a shout or a cry they
knelt, as with one accord, at the mouth of the precipice, with their backs to it, men and women and
children, knee to knee in a line, and joined hands,
and looked towards the soldiers, who were coming

steadily down on them. On and on the soldiers came, eye to eye with the people, and their swords were drawn. ·

Israel gasped for his breath, and waited to see the people cut in pieces at the next instant, when suddenly they began to sing where they knelt at the edge of the precipice, " God is our refuge and our strength, a very present help in trouble."

In another moment the soldiers had drawn up as if swords from heaven had fallen on them, and Israel was crying out of his dry throat, " Fear nothing! Only deliver your bodies to the Governor, and none shall harm you."

Then a terrible thing happened. Absalam rose up from his knees and called to his father and his son. And standing between them to be seen by all, and first looking upon both with eyes of pity, he drew from the folds of his selham a long knife such as the Reefians wear, and taking his father by his white hair he slew him and cast his body down the rocks. After that he turned towards his son, and the boy was golden-haired and his face was like the morning. Israel's heart bled to see him.

"Absalam," he cried in a moving voice, "Absalam, wait, wait!"

But Absalam killed his son also and cast him down after his father. Then, looking around on his people with eyes of compassion, as seeming to pity them that they must fall again into the hands of Israel and his master, he stretched out his knife and sheathed it in his own breast, and fell towards the precipice.

Israel covered his face and groaned in his heart, and said: "It is the end, O Lord God, it is the end—polluted wretch as I am, with the blood of these people upon me!"

The companions of Absalam delivered themselves to the soldiers, who committed them to the prison at Sháwan, and Ben Aboo went home in content.

Rumour of what had come to pass was not long in reaching Tetuan, and Israel was charged with the guilt of it. In passing through the streets the next day on his way to his house the people hissed him openly. "Allah had not written it!" a Moor shouted as he passed. "Take care!" cried an Arab, "Mohammed of Mequinez is coming!"

Now it chanced that night, after sundown, when Naomi, according to her wont, led her father to the upper room, and fetched the Book of the Law from the cupboard of the wall and laid it upon his knees, that he read the passage whereon the page opened of itself, scarce knowing what he read when he began to read it, for his spirit was heavy with the bad doings of those days. And the passage whereon the book opened was this—

"*Aaron shall cast lots upon the two goats: one lot for the Lord, and the other lot for the scapegoat. . . . Then shall he kill the goat of the sin-offering that is for the people, and bring his blood within the Vail, and he shall make an atonement for the holy place, because of the uncleanness of the children of Israel, and because of their transgressions in all their sins. . . . And when he hath made an end of reconciling the holy place, and the tabernacle of the congregation, and the altar, he shall bring the live goat, and Aaron shall lay both his hands upon the live goat, and confess over him all the iniquities of the children of Israel, and all their transgressions in all their sins, putting them upon the head of the goat, and shall send him away by the hand of a fit man into the wilderness. And the goat shall bear upon him all their iniquities into a land not inhabited."*

That same night Israel dreamt a dream. He had been asleep, and had awakened in a place which he did not know. It was a great arid wilderness. Ashen sand lay on every side; a scorching sun beat down on it, and nowhere was there a glint of water. Israel gazed, and slowly through the blazing sunlight he discerned white roofless walls like the ruins of little sheepfolds. "They are tombs," he told himself, "and this is a Mukabar—an Arab graveyard—the most desolate place in the world of God." But, looking again, he saw that the roofless walls covered the ground as far as the eye could see, and the thought came to him that this ashen desert was the earth itself, and that all the world of life and man was dead. Then, suddenly, in the motionless wilderness, a solitary creature moved. It was a goat, and it toiled over the hot sand with its head hung down and its tongue lolled out. "Water!" it seemed to cry, though it made no voice, and its eyes traversed the plain as if they would pierce the ground for a spring. Fever and delirium fell upon Israel. The goat came near to him and lifted up its eyes, and he saw its face. Then he shrieked and awoke. The face of the goat had been the face of Naomi.

Now Israel knew that this was no more than a dream, coming of the passage which he had read out of the book at sundown, but so vivid was the sense of it that he could not rest in his bed until he had first seen Naomi with his waking eyes, that he might laugh in his heart to think how the eye of his sleep had fooled him. So he lit his lamp and walked through the silent house to where Naomi's room was on the lower floor of it.

There she lay, sleeping so peacefully, with her

sunny hair flowing over the pillow on either side of her beautiful face, and rippling in little curls about her neck. How sweet she looked! How like a dear bud of womanhood just opening to the eye!

Israel sat down beside her for a moment. Many a time before, at such hours, he had sat in that same place, and then gone his ways, and she had known nothing of it. She was like any other maiden now. Her eyes were closed, and who should see that they were blind? Her breath came gently, and who should say that it gave forth no speech? Her face was quiet, and who should think that it was not the face of a homely hearted girl? Israel loved these moments when he was alone with Naomi while she slept, for then only did she seem to be entirely his own, and he was not so lonely while he was sitting there. Though men thought he was strong, yet he was very weak. He had no one in the world to talk to save Naomi, and she was dumb in the daytime, but in the night he could hold little conversations with her. His love! his dove! his darling! How

easily he could trick and deceive himself and think,
She will awake presently, and speak to me! Yes;
her eyes will open and see me here again, and I shall
hear her voice, for I love it! "Father!" she will
say. " Father—father——."

Only the moment of undeceiving was so cruel!

Naomi stirred, and Israel rose and left her. As
he went back to his bed, through the corridor of
the patio, he heard a night-cry behind him that
made his hair to rise. It was Naomi laughing in
her sleep.

Israel dreamt again that night, and he believed
his second dream to be a vision. It was only a
dream, like the first; but what his dream would be
to us is nought, and what it was to him is everything.
The vision as he thought he saw it was this, and
these were the words of it as he thought he heard
them—

It was the middle of the night, and he was lying
in his own room, when a dull red light as of dying
flame crossed the foot of the bed, and a voice that

was as the voice of the Lord came out of it, crying "Israel."

And Israel was sorely afraid and answered, "Speak, Lord, for thy servant heareth."

Then the Lord said, "Thou hast read of the goats whereon the high-priest cast lots, one lot for the sin-offering and one lot for the scapegoat."

And Israel answered trembling, "I have read."

Then the Lord said to Israel, "Look now upon Naomi, thy child, for she is as the sin-offering for thy sins, to make atonement for thy transgressions, for thee and for thy household, and therefore she is dumb to all uses of speech, and blind to all service of sight, a soul in chains and a spirit in prison, for behold, she is as the lot that is cast for justice and for the Lord."

And Israel groaned in his agony and cried, "Would that the lot had fallen upon me, O Lord, that thou mightest be justified when thou speakest, and be clear when thou judgest, for I alone am guilty before thee."

Then said the Lord to Israel, "On thee, also, hath the lot fallen, even the lot of the scapegoat of the enemies of the people of God."

And Israel quaked with fear, and the Lord called to him again, and said, "Israel, even as the scapegoat carries the iniquities of the people, so dost thou carry the iniquities of thy master, Ben Aboo, and of his wife, Katrina; and even as the goat bears the sins of the people into the wilderness, so, in the resurrection, shalt thou bear the sins of this man and of this woman into a land that no man knoweth."

Then Israel wrestled no longer with the Lord, but sweated as it were drops of blood, and cried, "What shall I do, O Lord?"

And the Lord said, "Lie unto the morning and then arise, get thee to the country by Mequinez and to the man there whereof thou hast heard tidings, and he shall show thee what thou shalt do."

Then Israel wept with gladness, and cried, saying, "Shall my soul live? Shall the lot be lifted from off me, and from off Naomi, my daughter?"

But the Lord left him, the red light died out from across the bed, and all around was darkness.

Now to the last day and hour of his life Israel would have taken oath on the Scriptures that he saw this vision, and heard this voice, not in his sleep and as in a dream, but awake, and having plain sight of all common things about him—his room and his bed, and the canopy that covered it. And on rising in the morning, at daydawn, so actual was the sense of what he had seen and heard, and so powerful the impression of it, that he straightway set himself to carry out the injunction it had made, without question of its reality or doubt of its authority.

Therefore, committing his household to the care of Ali, who was now grown to be a stalwart black lad, his constant right hand and helpmate, Israel first sent to the Governor, saying he should be ten days absent from Tetuan, and then to the Kasbah for a soldier and guide, and to the market-place for mules.

Before the sun was high everything was in readiness, and the caravan was waiting at the door. Then Israel remembered Naomi. Where was the girl that he had not seen her that morning ? They answered him that she had not yet left her room, and he sent the black woman Fatimah to fetch her. And when she came and he had kissed her, bidding her farewell in silence, his heart misgave him concerning her, and, after raising his foot to the stirrup, he returned to where she stood in the patio with the two bondwomen beside her.

" Is she well ? " he asked.

"Oh yes, well—very well," said Fatimah, and Habeebah echoed her. Nevertheless, Israel remembered that he had not heard the only language of her lips, her laugh, and, looking at her again, he saw that her face, which had used to be cheerful, was now sad. At that he almost repented of his purpose, and but for shame in his own eyes he might have gone no farther, for it smote him with terror that, though she were sick, nothing could she say to stay him, and even if she were dying she must let him go his ways without warning.

He kissed her again, and she clung to him, so that at last, with many words of tender protest which she did not hear, he had to break away from the beautiful arms that held him.

Ali was waiting by the mules in the streets, and the soldier and guide and muleteers and tentmen were already mounted, amid a chattering throng of idle people looking on.

" Ali, my lad," said Israel, " if anything should befall Naomi while I am away, will you watch over her and guard her with all your strength."

"With all my life," said Ali stoutly. He was Naomi's playfellow no longer, but her devoted slave.

Then Israel set off on his journey.

CHAPTER IX.

Now Mohammed of Mequinez, the man whom Israel went out to seek, was a Kádi and the son of a Kádi. While he was still a child his father died, and he was brought up by two uncles, his father's brothers, both men of yet higher place, the one being Náïb es-sultan, or Foreign Minister, at Tangier, and the other Grand Vizier to the Sultan, at Morocco. Thus in a land where there is one noble only, the Sultan himself, where ascent and descent are as free as in a Republic, though the ways of both are mired with crime and corruption, Mohammed was come as from the highest nobility. Nevertheless, he renounced his rank and the hope of wealth that went along with it at the call of duty and the cry of misery.

He parted from his uncles, abandoned his judge-ship, and went out into the plains. The poor and outcast and downtrodden among the people, the shamed, the disgraced, and the neglected left the towns and followed him. He established a sect. They were to be despisers of riches and lovers of poverty. No man among them was to have more than another. They were never to buy or sell among themselves, but every one was to give what he had to him that wanted it. They were to avoid swearing, yet whatever they said was to be firmer than an oath. They were to be ministers of peace, and if any man did them violence they were never to resist him. Nevertheless they were not to lack for courage, but to laugh to scorn the enemies that tormented them, and smile in their pains and shed no tear. And as for death, if it was for their glory they were to esteem it more than life, because their bodies only were corruptible, but their souls were immortal and would mount upwards when released from the bondage of the flesh. Not dissenters from the Koran, but stricter conformers to it; not Nazarenes and not Jews, yet followers of Jesus in their customs and of Moses in their doctrines.

And Moors and Berbers, Arabs and Negroes, Muslimeen and Jews heard the cry of Mohammed of Mequinez, and he received them all. From the streets, from the market-places, from the doors of the prisons, from the service of hard masters and from the ragged army itself, they arose in hundreds and trooped after him. They needed no badge but the badge of poverty, and no voice of pleading but the voice of misery. Most of them brought nothing with them in their hands, and some brought little on their backs save the stripes of their tormentors. A few had flocks and herds which they drove before them; a few had tents, which they shared with their fellows, and a few had guns with which they shot the wild boar for their food and the hyena for their safety. Thus, possessing little and desiring nothing, having neither houses nor lands, and only considering themselves secure from their rulers in having no money, this company of battered human wrecks, life-broken and crime-logged and stranded, passed with their leader from place to place of the waste country about Mequinez. And he, being as poor as they were, though he might have been so rich, cheered them always, even when they murmured against him, as Absalam had cheered his little fellowship at Tetuan : " God will feed us as He feeds the birds of the air, and clothe our little ones as He clothes the fields."

Such was the man whom Israel went out to seek. But Israel knew his people too well to make known his errand. His besetting difficulties were enough already. The year was young, but the days were hot; a palpitating haze floated always in the air, and the grass and the broom had the dusty and tired look of autumn. It was also the month of the fast of Ramadhán, and Israel's men were Muslims. So, to save himself the double vexation of oppressive days and the constant bickerings of his famished people, Israel found it necessary at length to travel in the night. In this way his journey was the shorter for the absence of some obstacles, but his time was long.

And, just as he had hidden his errand from the men of his own caravan, so he concealed it from the people of the country that he passed through, and many and various, and sometimes ludicrous and sometimes very pitiful, were the conjectures they made concerning it. While he was passing through his own province of Tetuan nothing did the poor people think but that he had come to make a new assessment of their lands and holdings, their cattle and belongings, that he might tax them afresh and more fully. So, to buy his mercy in advance, many of them came out of their houses as he drew near, and knelt on the ground before his horse, and kissed the skirts of his kaftan, and his knees, and even his foot in his stirrup, and called him *Sidi* (master, my lord), a title never before given to a Jew, and offered him presents out of their meagre substance.

"A gift for my lord," they would say, "of the

little that God has given us, praise His merciful
name for ever !"

Then they would push forward a sheep or a goat,
or a string of hens tied by the legs so as to hang
across his saddle-bow, or, perhaps, at the two
trembling hands of an old woman living alone on a
hungry scratch of land in a desolate place, a bowl of
buttermilk.

Israel was touched by the people's terror, but he
betrayed no feeling.

"Keep them," he would answer; "keep them
until I come again," intending to tell them, when
that time came. to keep their poor gifts altogether.

And when he had passed out of the province of
Tetuan into the bashalic of El Kasar, the bareheaded
country-people of the valley of the Koos hastened
before him to the Kaid of that grey town of bricks
and storks and palm-trees and evil odours, and the
Kaid, with another notion of his errand, came to
the tumble-down bridge to meet him on his approach
in the early morning.

"Peace be with you!" said the Kaid. "So my lord is going again to the Shereef at Wazzán; may the mercy of the Merciful protect him!"

Israel neither answered yea nor nay, but threaded the maze of crooked lanes to the lodging which had been provided for him near the market-place, and the same night he left the town (laden with the presents of the Kaid) through a line of famished and half-naked beggars who looked on with feverish eyes.

Next day, at dawn, he came to the heights of Wazzán (a holy city of Morocco) by the olives and junipers and evergreen oaks that grow at the foot of the lofty, double-peaked Boo-Hallal, and there the young Grand Shereef himself, at the gate of his odorous orange gardens, stood waiting to give audience with yet another conjecture as to the intention of his journey.

"Welcome! welcome!" said the Shereef; "all you see is yours until Allah shall decree that you leave me too soon on your happy mission to our lord the Sultan at Fez—may God prolong his life and bless him!"

"God make you happy!" said Israel; but he offered no answer to the question that was implied.

"It is twenty and odd years, my lord," the Shereef continued, "since my father sent for you out of Tetuan, and many are the ups and downs that time has wrought since then, under Allah's will; but none in the past have been so grateful as the elevation of Israel ben Oliel, and none in the future can be so joyful as the favours which the Sultan (God keep our lord Abd er-Rahman!) has still in store for him.

"God will show," said Israel.

No Jew had ever yet ridden in this Moroccan Mecca; but the Shereef alighted from his horse and offered it to Israel, and took Israel's horse instead, and together they rode through the market-place, and past the old Mosque that is a ruin inhabited by hawks, and the other mosque of the Aïssáwà, and the three squalid fondaks wherein the Jews live like cattle. A swarm of Arabs followed at their heels in tattered and greasy rags, a group of Jews went by them barefoot, and a knot of bedraggled renegades leaning against the walls of the prison doffed the caps from their dishevelled heads and bowed.

That day, while the poor people of the town fasted according to the ordinance of the Ramadhán, Israel's little company of Muslimeen—guests in the house of the descendants of the Prophet—were, by special Shereefian dispensation, permitted as travellers to eat and drink at their pleasure. And before sunset, but at the verge of it, Israel and his men started on their journey afresh, going out of the town, with the Shereef's black bodyguard riding before them for guide and badge of honour, through the dense and noisome market-place, where (like a clock that is warning to strike) a multitude of hungry and thirsty people with fierce and dirty faces, under a heavy wave of palpitating heat, and amid clouds of hot dust, were waiting for the sound of the cannon that should proclaim the end of that day's fast. Water-carriers at the fountains stood ready to fill their empty goats' skins, women and children sat on the ground with dishes of greasy soup on their knees and balls of grain rolled in their fingers, men lay about holding pipes charged with keef, and flint and tinder to light them, and the mueddin himself in the minaret, stood looking abroad (unless he were blind) to where the red sun was lazily sinking under the plain.

Israel's soul sickened within him, for well he knew that, lavish as were the honours that were shown him, they were offered by the rich out of their selfishness and by the poor out of their fear. While they thought the Sultan had sent for him they kissed his foot who desired no homage, and loaded him with presents who needed no gifts. But one word out of his mouth, only one little word, one other name, and what then of this lip-service, and what of this mock-honour!

Two days later Israel and his company reached before dawn the snake-like ramparts of Mequinez, the city of walls. And toiling in the darkness over the barren plain and the belt of carrion that lies in front of the town, through the heat and fumes of the fetid place, and amid the furious barks of the scavenger dogs which prowl in the night around it, they came in the grey of morning to the city gate over the stream called the Father of Tortoises. The gate was closed and the night police that kept it were snoring in their rags, under the arch of the wall within.

"Selám! M·barak! Abd el Káder! Abd el Kareem!" shouted the Shereef's black guard to the sleepy gate-keepers. They had come thus far in Israel's honour and would not return to Wazzán until they had seen him housed within.

From the other side of the gate, through the mist and the gloom, came yawns and broken snores and then snarls and curses. "Burn your father! Pretty hubbub in the middle of the night!"

"Selám!" shouted one of the black guard. "You dog of dogs! Your father was bewitched by a hyena! I'll teach you to curse your betters. Quick! Get up, or I'll shave your beard. Open! Or I'll ride the donkey on your head! There!—and there!—and

there again!" and at every word the butt of his long
gun rang on the old oaken gate.

"Hamed el Wazzáni!" muttered several voices
within.

"Yes," shouted the Shereef's man. "And my
Lord Israel of Tetuan on his way to the Sultan, God
grant him victory. Do you hear, you dogs? Sidi
Israel el Tetáwani sitting here in the dark, while you
are sleeping and snoring in your dirt."

There was a whispered conference on the inside,
then a rattle of keys, and then the gate groaned back
on its hinges. At the next moment two of the four
gatemen were on their knees at the feet of Israel's
horse, asking forgiveness by grace of Allah and his
Prophet. In the meantime, the other two had sped
away to the Kasbah, and before Israel had ridden far
into the town, the Kaid—against all usage of his
class and country—ran and met him—afoot, slipper-
less, wearing nothing but selham and tarboosh, out
of breath, yet with a mouth full of excuses.

"I heard you were coming," he panted—"sent for

by the Sultan—Allah preserve him!—but had I known you were to be here so soon—I—that is——"

"Peace be with you!" interrupted Israel.

"God grant you peace. The Sultan—praise the merciful Allah!" the Kaid continued, bowing low over Israel's stirrup—"he reached Fez from Marrâkesh last sunset; you will be in time for him."

"God will show," said Israel, and he pushed forward.

"Ah, true—yes—certainly—my lord is tired," puffed the Kaid, bowing again most profoundly. "Well, your lodging is ready—the best in Mequinez—and your mona is cooking—all the dainties of Barbary—and when our merciful Abd er-Rahman has made you his Grand Vizier——"

Thus the man chattered like a jay, bowing low at nigh every word, until they came to the house wherein Israel and his people were to rest until sunset; and always the burden of his words was the same—the Sultan, the Sultan, the Sultan, and Abd er-Rahman, Abd er-Rahman!

Israel could bear no more. "Basha," he said, "it is a mistake; the Sultan has not sent for me, and neither am I going to see him."

"Not going to him?" the Kaid echoed vacantly.

"No, but to another," said Isra.l, "and you of all men can best tell me where that other is to be found. A great man, newly risen—yet a poor man—the young Mahdi Mohammed of Mequinez."

Then there was a long silence.

Israel did not rest in Mequinez until sunset of that day. Soon after sunrise he went out at the gate at which he had so lately entered, and no man showed him honour. The black guard of the Shereef of Wazzán had gone off before him, chuckling and grinning in their disgust, and behind him his own little company of soldiers, guides, muleteers, and tent-men, who, like himself, had neither slept nor eaten, were dragging along in dudgeon. The Kaid had turned them out of the town.

Later in the day, while Israel and his people lay sheltering within their tents on the plain of Saïs,

by the river Nagar, near the tent-village called a
Douar, and the palm-tree by the bridge, there passed
them in the fierce sunshine two men in the peaked
shasheeah of the soldier, riding at a furious gallop
from the direction of Fez, and shouting to all they
came upon to fly from the path they had to pass over.
They were messengers of the Sultan, carrying letters
to the Kaid of Mequinez, commanding him to present
himself at the palace without delay, that he might
give good account of his stewardship, or else deliver
up his substance and be cast into prison for the
defalcations with which rumour had charged him.

Such was the errand of the soldiers, according to
the country-people, who toiled along after them on
their way home from the markets at Fez; and great
was the glee of Israel's men on hearing it, for they
remembered with bitterness how basely the Kaid had
treated them at last in his false loyalty and hypocrisy.
But Israel himself was too nearly touched by a sense
of Fate's coquetry to rejoice at this new freak of its
whim, though the victim of it had so lately turned

him from his door. Miserable was the man who laid up his treasure in money-bags and built his happiness on the favour of princes! When the one was taken from him and the other failed him, where then was the hope of that man's salvation, whether in this world or the next? The dungeon, the chain, the lash, the wooden jellab—what else was left to him? Only the wail of the poor whom he has made poorer, the curse of the orphan whom he has made fatherless, and the execration of the down-trodden whom he has oppressed. These followed him into his prison, and mingled their cries with the clank of his irons, for they were voices which had never yet deserted the man that made them, but clamoured loud at the last when his end had come, above the death-rattle in his throat. One dim hour waited for all men always, whether in the prison or in the palace—one lonely hour wherein none could bear him company—and what was wealth and treasure to man's soul beyond it? Was it power on earth? Was it glory? Was it riches? Oh! glory of the earth—what could it be but a will-o'-the-wisp pursued in the darkness of the night! Oh! riches of gold and silver—what had they ever been but marsh-fire gathered in the dusk! The empire of the world was evil, and evil was the service of the prince of it!

Then Israel thought of Naomi, his sweet treasure so far away. Though all else fell from him like dry sand from graspless fingers, yet if by God's good mercy the lot of the sin-offering could be lifted away from his child he would be content and happy. Naomi! His love! His darling! His sweet flower afflicted for his transgression. Oh! let him lose anything, everything, all that the world and all that the devil had given him; but let the curse be lifted from his helpless child! For what was gold without gladness, and what was plenty without peace?

Israel lit upon the Mahdi at last in the country of the verbena and the musk that lies outside the walls of Fez. The prophet was a young man of unusual stature, but no great strength of body, with a head that drooped like a flower and with the wild eyes of an enthusiast. His people were a vast concourse that covered the plain a furlong square, and included multitudes of women and children. Israel had come upon them at an evil moment. The people were murmuring against their leader. Six months ago they had abandoned their houses and followed him. They had passed from Mequinez to Rabat, from Rabat to Mazagan, from Mazagan to Mogador, from Mogador to Marrákesh, and finally from Marrákesh through the treacherous Beni Magild to Fez. At every step their numbers had increased but their substance had diminished, for only the destitute had joined them. Nevertheless, while they had their flocks and herds they had borne their privations patiently—the weary journeys, the exposure, the long rains of the spring and the scorching heat of summer. But the soldiers of the Kaids whose provinces they had passed through had stripped them of both in the name of tribute. The last raid on their poverty had been made that very day by the Kaid of Fez, and now they were without

goats or sheep or oxen, or even the guns with which
they had killed the wild boar, and their children
were crying to them for bread.

So the people's faces grew black, and they looked
into each other's eyes in their impotent rage. Why
had they been brought out of the cities to starve?
Better to stay there and suffer than come out and
perish! What of the vain promises that had been
made to them that God would feed them as He fed
the birds! God was witness to all their calamities;
He was seeing them robbed day by day, He was
seeing them famish hour by hour, He was seeing
them die. They had been fooled! A vain man had
thought to plough his way to power. Through
their bodies he was now ploughing it. "The hunger
is on us!" "Our children are perishing!" "Find
us food!" "Food!" "Food!"

With such shouts, mingled with deep oaths, the
hungry multitude in their madness had encompassed
Mohammed of Mequinez as Israel and his company
came up with them. And Israel heard their cries,

and also the voice of their leader when he answered them.

And first the young prophet rose up among his people, with flashing eyes and quivering nostrils. "Do you think I am Moses," he cried, "that I should smite the rock and work you a miracle! If you are starving, am I full? If you are naked, am I clothed?"

But in another instant the fire of anger was gone from his face, and he was saying in a very moving voice, "My good people, who have followed me through all these miseries, I know that your burdens are heavier than you can bear, and that your lives are scarce to be endured, and that death itself would be a relief. Nevertheless, who shall say but that Allah sees a way to avert these trials of His poor servants, and that, unknown to us all, He is even at this moment bringing His mercy to pass! Patience, I beg of you; patience, my poor people— patience and trust!"

At that the murmurs of discontent were hushed,

Then Israel remembered the presents with which the Kaid of El Kasar and the Shereef of Wazzán had burdened him. They were jewels and ornaments such as are sometimes worn unlawfully by vain men in that country—silver signet rings and earrings, chains for the neck, and Solomon's seal to hang on the breast as safeguard against the evil eye—as well as much gold filagree of the kind that men give to their women. Israel had packed them in a box and laid them in the leaf pannier of a mule and then given no further thought to them; but, calling now to the muleteer who had charge of them, he said, "Take them quickly to the good man yonder, and say, 'A present to the man of God and to his people in their trouble.'"

And when the muleteer had done this, and laid the box of gold and silver open at the feet of the young Mahdi, saying what Israel had bidden him, it was the same to the young man and his followers as if the sky had opened and rained manna on their heads. "It is an answer to your prayer,"

he cried; "an angel from heaven has sent it."
Then his people, as soon as they realised what
good thing had happened to them, took up his
shout of joy, and shouted out of their own parched
throats, "Prophet of Allah, we will follow you to the
world's end!" And then, down to their knees they
fell around him, the vast concourse of men and
women, all grinning like apes in their hunger and
glee together, and sobbing and laughing in a breath,
like children, and sent up a great broken cry of thanks
to God that He had sent them succour, that they
might not die. At last, when they had risen to
their feet again, every man looked into the eyes of
his fellow, and said, as if ashamed, "I could have
borne it myself, but when the children called to me
for bread, I was a fool."

CHAPTER X.

THE next day thereafter Israel set his face homeward, with this old word of the new prophet for his
guide and motto: " Exact no more than is just; do
violence to no man; accuse none falsely; part with
your riches and give to the poor." That was all the
answer he got out of his journey, and if any man had
come to him in Tetuan with no newer story, it must
have been an idle and a foolish errand; but after
El Kasar, after Wazzán, after Mequinez, and now
after Fez, it seemed to be the sum of all wisdom.
"I'll do it," he said; "at all risks and all costs I'll
do it."

And, as a prelude to that change in his way
of life which he meant to bring to pass, he sent
forward his men and mules ahead of him, emptied

his pockets of all that he should not need on his journey, and prepared to return to his own country on foot and alone. The men had first gaped in amazement, and then laughed in derision; and finally they had gone their ways by themselves, telling all who encountered them that the Sultan at Fez had stripped their master of everything, and that he was coming behind them penniless.

But, knowing nothing of this graceless service, Israel began on his homeward journey with a happy heart. He had less than thirty dollars in his waist-band of the more than three hundred with which he had set out from Tetuan; he was a hundred and fifty miles from that town, or five long days' travel; the sun was still hot, and he must walk in the day-time. Surely the Lord would see it that never before had any man done so much to wipe out God's dis-pleasure as he was now doing and yet would do. He had said nothing of Naomi to the Mahdi even when he told him of his vision; but all his hopes had centred in the child. The lot of the sin-offering must be gone from her now, and in the resurrection he would meet her without shame. If he had brought fruits meet to repentance, then must her debt also be wiped away. Surely never before had any child been so smitten of God, and never had any father of an afflicted child bought God's mercy at so dear a price!

Such were the thoughts that Israel cherished secretly, though he dared not to utter them lest he should seem to be bribing God out of his love of the child. And thus if his heart was glad as he turned towards home, it was proud also, and if it was grateful it was also vain; but vanity and pride were both smitten out of it in an hour, before he went through the gates of Fez (wherein he had slept the night preceding), by three sights which, though stern and pitiful, were of no uncommon occurrence in that town and province.

First, it chanced that as he was passing from the south-east of the new town of Fez to the gate that is at the north-west corner, going by the high walls of the Sultan's harem, where there is room for a

thousand women, and near to the Karueeïn mosque
that is the greatest in Morocco and rests on eight
hundred pillars, he came upon two slaveholders selling
twelve or fourteen slaves. The slaves were all girls,
and all black, and of varying ages, ranging from ten
years to about thirty. They had lately arrived in
caravans from the Soudan, by way of Tafilelt and
the Waghar, and some of them looked worn from the
desert passage. Others were fresh and cheerful, and
such as had claims to negro beauty were adorned,
after their doubtful fashion, or the fancy of their
masters, with love-charms of silver, worn about their
necks, with their fingers pricked out with hennah,
and their eyelids darkened with kohl. Thus they
were drawn up in a line for public auction; but before
the sale of them could begin among the buyers that
had gathered about them in the street, the overseers
of the Sultan's hareem had to come and make a selec-
tion for their master. This the eunuchs presently
did, and when two of them nicknamed Âreefahs—
gaunt and hairless men, with the faces of evil old

women and the hoarse voices of ravens—had picked out three fat black maidens, the business of the auction began by the sale of a negro girl of seventeen who was brought out from the rest and passed around.

Israel's blood tingled to see how the bidders handled the girl, and to hear what shameless questions they asked of her, and with a long sigh he was turning away from the crowd, when another man came up to it. The man was black and old and hard-featured, and visibly poor in his torn white selham. But when he had looked over the heads of those in front of him, he made a great shout of anguish, and, parting the people, pushed his way to the girl's side, and opened his arms to her, and she fell into them with a cry of joy and pain together.

It turned out that he was a liberated slave, who, ten years before, had been brought from the Soos through the country of Sidi Hasham ben Hosaïn, having been torn away from his wife, who was since dead, and from his only child, who thus strangely rejoined him. This story he told, in broken Arabic, to those that stood around, and, hard as were the faces of the bidders, and brutal as was their trade, there was not an eye among them all but was melted at his story.

Seeing this, Israel cried from the back of the crowd, "I will give twenty dollars to buy him the girl's liberty," and straightway another and another offered like sums for the same purpose until the amount of the last bid had been reached, and the slave-master took it, and the girl was free. Then the poor negro, still holding his daughter by the hand, came to Israel, with the tears dripping down his black cheeks, and said in his broken way: "The blessing of Allah upon you, white brother, and if you have a child of your own may you never lose her, but may Allah favour her and let you keep her with you always!"

That blessing of the old black man was more than Israel could bear, and, facing about before hearing the last of it, he turned down the dark arcade that descends

into tne old town as into a vault, and having crossed
the markets, he came upon the second of the three
sights that were to smite out of his heart his pride
towards God. A man in a blue tunic girded with a
red sash, and with a red cotton handkerchief tied about
his head, was driving a donkey laden with trunks of
light trees cut into short lengths to lie over its panniers.
He was clearly a Spanish woodseller, and he had the
weary, averted, and downcast look of a race that is
despised and kept under. His donkey was a bony
creature, with raw places on its flank and shoulders
where its hide had been worn by the friction of its
burdens. He drove it slowly, crying "Arrah!" to
it in the tongue of its own country, and not beating
it cruelly. At the bottom of the arcade there was
an open place where a foul ditch was crossed
by a rickety bridge. Coming to this the man
hesitated a moment, as if doubtful whether to drive
his donkey over it or to make the beast trudge
through the water. Concluding to cross the bridge
he cried "Arrah!" again, and drove the donkey

forward with one blow of his stick. But when the donkey was in the middle of it the rotten thing gave way, and the beast and its burden fell into the ditch. The donkey's legs were broken, and when a throng of Arabs, who gathered at the Spaniard's cry, had cut away its panniers and dragged it out of the water on to the paving stones of the street, the film covered its eyes, and in a moment it was dead.

At that the man knelt down beside it, and patted it on its neck and called on it by its name, as if unwilling to believe that it was gone. And while the Arabs laughed at him for doing so—for none seemed to pity him—a slatternly girl of sixteen or seventeen came scudding down the arcade, and pushing her way through the crowd until she stood where the dead ass lay with the man kneeling beside it. Then she fell on the man with bitter reproaches. "Allah blot out your name, you thief!" she cried. "You've killed the creature, and may you starve and die yourself, you dog of a Nazarene!"

This was more than Israel could listen to, and he

commanded the girl to hold her peace. "Silence, you young wanton!" he cried, in a voice of indignation. "Who are you that you dare trample on the man in his trouble?"

It turned out that the girl was the man's daughter, and he was a renegade from Ceuta. And when she had gone off, cursing Israel and his father and his grandfather, the poor fellow lifted his eyes to Israel's face, and said, "You are very kind, my father. God bless you! I may not be a good man, sir, and I've not lived a right life, but it's hard when your own children are taught to despise you. Better to lose them in their cradles, before they can speak to you to curse you."

Israel's hair seemed to rise from his scalp at that word, and he turned about and hurried away. Oh no, no, no! He was not, of all men, the most sorely tried. Worse to be a slave, torn from the arms he loves! Worse to be a father whose children join with his enemies to curse him!

He had been wrong. What was wealth that it was

so noble a sacrifice to part with it? Money was to give and to take, to buy and to sell, and that was all. But love was for no market, and he who lost it lost everything. And love was his, and would be his always, for he loved Naomi, and she clung to him as the hyssop clings to the wall. Let him walk humbly before God, for God was great.

Now these sights, though they reduced Israel's pride, increased his cheerfulness, and he was going out at the gate with a humbler yet lighter spirit, when he came upon a saint's house under the shadow of the town walls. It was a small whitewashed enclosure, surmounted by a white flag; and, as Israel passed it, the figure of a man came out to the entrance. He was a poor, miserable creature—ragged, dirty, and with dishevelled hair—and, seeing Israel's eyes upon him, he began to talk in some wild way and unknown tongue that was only a fierce jabber of sounds that had no words in them, and of words that had no meaning. The poor soul was mad, and because he was distraught he was counted a holy man among his people, and put to live in this place, which was the tomb of a dead saint: though not more dead to the ways of life was he who lay under the floor than he who lived above it. The man continued his wild jabber as long as Israel's eyes were on him, and Israel dropped two crowns into his hand and passed on.

Oh no, no, no; Naomi was not the most afflicted of all God's creatures. And yet, and yet, and yet, her bodily infirmities were but the type and sign of how her soul was smitten.

On the hill outside the town the young Mahdi, with a great company of his people, was waiting for him to bid him godspeed on his journey. And then, while they walked some paces together before parting, and the prophet talked of the poor followers of Absalam lying in the prison at Shâwan (for he had heard of them from Israel), Israel himself mentioned Naomi.

"My father," he said, "there is something that I have not told you."

"Tell it now, my son," said the Mahdi.

"I have a little daughter at home, and she is very sweet and beautiful. You would never think how like sunshine she is to me in my lonely house, for her mother is gone, and but for her I should be alone, and so she is very near and dear to me. But she is in the land of silence and in the land of night. Nothing can she see, and nothing hear, and never has her voice opened the curtains of the air, for she is blind and dumb and deaf."

"Merciful Allah!" cried the Mahdi.

"Ah! is her state so terrible? I thought you would think it so. Yes, for all she is so beautiful, she is only as a creature of the fields that knows not God."

"Allah preserve her!" cried the Mahdi.

"And she is smitten for my sin, for the Lord revealed it to me in the vision, and my soul trembles for her soul. But if God has washed me with water should not she also be clean?"

"God knows," said the Mahdi. "He gives no rewards for repentance."

"But listen!" said Israel. "In a vision of death her mother saw her and she was afflicted no more. No, for she could see, and hear, and speak. Man of God, will it come to pass?"

"God is good," said the Mahdi. "He needs that no man should teach Him pity."

"But I love her," cried Israel, "and I vowed to her mother to guard her. She is joy of my joy and life of my life. Without her the morning has no freshness and the night no rest. Surely the Lord sees this, and will have mercy?"

The Mahdi held back his tears, and answered, "The Lord sees all. Go your way in trust. Farewell!"

"Farewell!"

CHAPTER XI.

ISRAEL'S return home was an experience at all points the reverse of his going abroad. He had seven dollars in the pocket of his waistband on setting away from Fez, out of the three hundred and more with which he had started from Tetuan. His men had gone on before him and told their story. So the people whom he came upon by the way either ignored him or jeered at him, and not one that on his coming had run to do him honour now stepped aside that he might pass.

Two days after leaving Fez he came again to Wazzán. Women were going home from market by the side of their camels, and charcoal-burners were riding back to the country on the empty burdas of their mules. It was nigh upon sunset when Israel

entered the town, and so exactly was everything the
same that he could almost have tricked himself and
believed that scarce two minutes had passed since he
had left it. There at the fountains were the water-
carriers waiting with their water-skins, and there in
the market-place sat the women and children with
their dishes of soup; there were the men by the
booths with their pipes ready charged with keef, and
there was the mooddin in the minaret, looking out
over the plain. Everything was the same save one
thing, and that concerned Israel himself. No Grand
Shereef stood waiting to exchange horses with him,
and no black guard led him through the town. Foot-
sore and dirty, covered with dust, and tired, he
walked through the streets alone. And when presently the voice rang out overhead, and the breathless town broke instantly into bubbles of sounds—the
tinkling of the bells of the water-carriers, the shouts
of the children, and the calls of the men—only one
man seemed to see him and know him. This was an
Arab, wearing scarcely enough rags to cover his

nakedness, who was bathing his hot cheeks in water which a water-carrier was pouring into his hands, and he lifted his glistening face as Israel passed, and called him "Dog!" and "Jew!" and commanded him to uncover his feet.

Israel slept that night in one of the three squalid fondaks of Wazzán inhabited by the Jews. His room was a sort of narrow box, in a square court of many such boxes, with a handful of straw shaken over the earth floor for a bed. On the doorpost the figure of a hand was painted in red, and over the lintel there was a rude drawing of a scorpion, with an impreca-tion written under it that purported to be from the mouth of the Prophet Joshua, son of Nun. If the charm kept evil spirits from the place of Israel's rest, it did not banish good ones. Israel slept in that poor bed as he had never slept under the purple canopy of his own chamber, and all night long one angel form seemed to hover over him. It was Naomi. He could see her clearly. They were together in a little cottage somewhere. The house was a mean one, but

jasmine and marjoram and pinks and roses grew
outside of it, and love grew inside. And Naomi!
How bright were her eyes, for they could see! Yes,
and her ears could hear, and her tongue could speak!

Two days after Israel left Wazzán he was back in
the Bashalic of Tetuan. Each night he had dreamt
the same dream, and though he knew each morning
when he awoke with a sigh that his dream was only
a reflection of his dead wife's vision, yet he could not
help but think of it the long day through. He tried
to remember if he had ever seen the cottage with his
waking eyes, and where he had seen it, and to recall
the voice of Naomi as he had heard it in his dream,
that he might know if it was the same as he used to
think he heard when he sat by her in his stolen
watches of the night while she lay asleep. Sometimes
when he reflected he thought he must be growing
childish, so foolish was his joy in looking forward to
the night—for he had almost grown in love with it—
that he might dream his dream again.

But it was a dear, delicious folly, for it helped him

to bear the troubles of his journey, and they were neither light nor few. After passing through El Kasar he had been robbed and stripped both of his small remaining moneys and the better part of his clothes by a gang of ruffians who had followed him out of the town. Then a good woman—the old wife turned into the servant of a Moor who had married a young one—had taken pity on his condition and given him a disused Moorish jellab. His misfortune had not been without its advantage. Being forced to travel the rest of his way home in the disguise of a Moor, he had heard himself discussed by his own people when they knew nothing of his presence. Every evil that had befallen them had been attributed to him. Ben Aboo, their Basha, was a good humane man, who was often driven to do that which his soul abhorred. It was Israel ben Oliel who was their cruel taxmaster.

When Israel was within a day's journey of Tetuan a terrible scourge fell upon the country. A plague of locusts came up like a dense cloud from the

direction of the desert and ate up every leaf and blade
of grass that the scorching sun had left green, so that
the plain over which it had passed was as black and
barren as a lava stream. The farmers were im-
poverished, and the poorer people made beggars.
Even this last disaster they charged in their despair
to Israel, for Allah was now cursing them for Israel's
sake. They were the same people that had thrust
their presents upon him when he was setting out.

At the lonesome hut of the old woman who had
offered him a bowl of buttermilk, Israel rested and
asked for a drink of water. She gave him a dish of
zummeeta—barley roasted like coffee—and inquired
if he was going on to Tetuan. He told her yes,
and she asked if his home was there. And when he
answered that it was, she looked at him again, and
said in a moving way, "Then Allah help you,
brother."

" Why me more than another, sister ? " said
Israel.

" Because it is plain to see that you are a poor

man," said the old woman. "And that is the sort he is hardest upon."

Israel faltered and said, "He? Who, mother? Ah, you mean——"

"Who else but Israel, the Jew?" said she; and then added, as by a sudden afterthought, "But they say he is gone at last, and the Sultan has stripped him. Well, Allah send us some one else soon to set right this poor Gharb of ours! And what a man for poor men he might have been—so wise and powerful!"

Israel listened with his head bent down, and, like a moth at the flame, he could not help but play with the fire that scorched him. "They tell me," he said, "that Allah has cursed him with a daughter that has devils."

"Blind and dumb, poor soul," said the old woman; "but Allah has pity for the afflicted—he is taking her away."

Israel rose. "Away?"

"She is ill since her father went to Fez."

" Ill ? "

" Yes, I heard so, yesterday—dying."

Israel made one loud cry like the cry of a beast
that is slaughtered, and fled out of the hut.   Oh, fool
of fools, why had he been dallying with dreams—
billing and cooing with his own fancies—fondling
and nuzzling and coddling them ?   Let all dreams
henceforth be dead and damned for ever; for only
devils out of hell had made them that poor men's
souls might be staked and lost !   Oh, why had he
not remembered the pale face of Naomi when he left
her, and the silence of her tongue that had used to
laugh ?   Fool, fool !   Why had he ever left her at
all ?

With such thoughts Israel hurried along, sometimes running at his utmost velocity, and then
stopping dead short; sometimes shouting his impre-
cations at the pitch of his voice and beating his fist
against the sharp aloes until it bled, and then
whispering to himself in awe.

Would God not hear his prayer?   God knew the

child was very near and dear to him, and also that he was a lonely man. "Have pity on a lonely man, O God!" he whispered. " Let me keep my child ; take all else that I have, everything, no matter what! Only let me keep her—yes, just as she is, let me have her still! Time was when I asked more of Thee, but now I am humble, and ask that alone."

On his knees in a lonesome place, with the fierce sun beating down on his uncovered head, amid the blackened leaves left by the locust, he prayed this prayer, and then rose to his feet and ran.

When he got to Tetuan the white city was glistening under the setting sun. Then he thought of his Moorish jellab, and looked at himself, and saw that he was returning home like a beggar ; and he remembered with what splendour he had started out. Should he wait for the darkness, and creep into his house under the cover of it? If the thought had occurred an hour before he must have scouted it. Better to brave the looks of every face in Tetuan than be kept back one minute from Naomi. But now that he was so near he was afraid to go in ; and now that he was so soon to learn the truth he dreaded to hear it. So he walked to and fro on the heath outside the town, paltering with himself, struggling with himself, eating out his heart with eagerness, trying to believe that he was waiting for the night.

The night came at length, and, under a deep-blue sky fast whitening with thick stars, Israel passed unknown through the Moorish gate, which was still open, and down the narrow lane to the market square. At the gate of the Mellah, which was closed, he knocked, and demanded entrance in the name of the Kaid. The Moorish guards who kept it fell back at sight of him with looks of consternation.

" Israel ! " cried one, and dropped his lantern.

Israel whispered, " Keep your tongue between your teeth ! " and hurried on.

At the door of his own house, which was also closed, he knocked again, but more fearfully. The black woman Habeebah opened it cautiously, and, seeing his jellab, she clashed it back in his face.

"Habeebah!" he cried, and he knocked once more.

Then Ali came to the door. "What Moorish man are you?" cried Ali, pushing him back as he pressed forward.

"Ali! Hush! It is I—Israel."

Then Ali knew him and cried, "God save us! What has happened?"

"What has happened here?" said Israel. "Naomi," he faltered, "what of her?"

"Then you have heard?" said Ali. "Thank God she is now well."

Israel laughed—his laugh was like a scream.

"More than that—a strange thing has befallen her since you went away," said Ali.

"What?"

"She can hear."

"It's a lie!" cried Israel, and he raised his hand and struck Ali to the floor. But at the next minute he was lifting him up and sobbing and saying, "Forgive me, my brave boy. I was mad, my son; I did not know what I was doing.   But do not torture me.   If what you tell me is true, there is no man so happy under heaven; but if it is false, there is no fiend in hell need envy me."

And Ali answered through his tears, "It is true, my father—come and see."

CHAPTER XII.

WHAT had happened at Israel's house during Israel's absence is a story that may be quickly told. On the day of his departure Naomi wandered from room to room, seeming to seek for what she could not find, and in the evening the black women came upon her in the upper chamber wherein her father had read to her at sunset, and she was kneeling by his chair and the book was in her hands.

On the day following she stole out of the house into the town and made her way to the Kasbah, and Ali found her in the apartments of the wife of the Basha, who had lit upon her as she seemed to ramble aimlessly through the courtyard from the Treasury to the Hall of Justice, and from there to the gate of the prison.

The next day after that she did not attempt to go
abroad, and neither did she wander through the
house, but sat in the same seat constantly, and
seemed to be waiting patiently. She was pale and
quiet and silent; she did not laugh according to her
wont, and she had a look of submission that was
very touching to see.

On the morning of the day following that, her
quiet had given place to restlessness, and her pallor
to a burning flush of the face. Her hands were hot,
her head was feverish, and her blind eyes were
bloodshot.

It was now plain that the girl was ill, and that
Israel's fears on setting out from home had been
right after all. And making his own reckoning with
Naomi's condition, Ali went off for the only doctor
living in Tetuan—a Spanish druggist living in the
walled lane leading to the western gate. This good
man came to look at Naomi, felt her pulse, touched
her throbbing forehead, with difficulty examined her
tongue, and pronounced her illness to be fever. He

gave some homely directions as to her treatment —
for he despaired of administering drugs to such a
one as she was—and promised to return the next
day.

About the middle of that night Naomi became
delirious. Fatimah stood constantly by her bed,
bathing her hot forehead with vinegar and water;
Habeebah slept in a chair at her feet; and Ali
crouched in a corner outside the door of her room.

The druggist came in the morning, according to
his promise; but there was nothing to be done, so he
looked wise, wagged his head very solemnly, and said
he would come again after two days more, when the
fever must be near to its height, and bring a famous
leech out of Tangier along with him.

Meantime, Naomi's delirium continued. It was
gentle as her own spirit, but there was this that was
strange and eerie about her unconsciousness—that
whereas she had been dumb while her mind in its
dark cell must have been mistress of itself and of her
soul, she spoke without ceasing throughout the time

of her reason's vanquishment. Not that her poor tongue in its trouble uttered speech such as those that heard could follow and understand, but only a restless babble of empty sounds, yet with tones of varying feeling, sometimes of gladness, sometimes of sorrow, sometimes of remonstrance, and sometimes of entreaty.

All that night and the next night also the two black women sat together by her bedside, holding each other's hands like little children in great fear. Also Ali crouched again like a dog in the darkness outside the door, listening in terror to the silvery young voice that had never echoed in that house before. This was the night when Israel, sleeping at the squalid inn of the Jews of Wazzán, was hearing Naomi's voice in his dreams.

At the first glint of daylight in the morning the lad was up and gone, and away through the town-gate to the heath beyond, as far as to the fondak, which stands on the hill above it, that he might strain his wet eyes in the pitiless sunlight for Israel's caravan that should soon come. On the first morning he saw nothing, but on the second morning he came upon Israel's men returning without him, and telling their lying story that he had been stripped of everything by the Sultan at Fez, and was coming behind them penniless.

Now, Israel was to Ali the greatest, noblest, mightiest man among men. That he should fall was incredible, and that any man should say he had fallen was an affront and an outrage. So, stripling as he was, the lad faced the rascals with the courage of a lion. They were liars and thieves, they were villains; let them tell that story to another soul in Tetuan, and he would go straight to the Kaid at the Kasbah, and have every black dog of them all whipped through the streets for plundering his master!

The men shouted in derision and passed on, firing their matchlocks as a mock salute. But Ali had his will of them; they told their tale no more, and when they entered Tetuan, and their fellows questioned them concerning their journey, they took refuge in the reticence that sits by right of nature on the tongues of Moors, and they said and knew nothing.

While Ali was on the heath looking out for Israel, the doctor out of Tangier came to Naomi. The girl was still unconscious, and the wise leech shook his head over her. Her case was hopeless; she was sinking—in plain words, she was dying, and if her father did not come before the morrow he would come too late to find her alive.

Then the black women fell to weeping and wailing, and after that to spiritual conflict. Both were born in Islam, but Fatimah had secretly become a Jewess by persuasion of her mistress, who was dead. She was, therefore, for sending for the Chacham. But Habeebah had remained a Muslim, and she was for calling the Imâm. The Imâm was good, the Imâm was holy; who so good and holy as the Imâm? Nay, but their Sidi held not with the Imâm, for their lord was a Jew, and their lord was their master, their lord was their sultan, their lord was their king. Shoof! What was Sidi against paradise, and paradise was to her who made a follower of Moosa into a follower of Mohammed? Let but the child die with the Kelmah on her lips, and they were all three blest for ever—otherwise, they would burn everlastingly in the fires of Jehinnum! But, alack! how could the poor girl say the Kelmah, being as dumb as the grave? Then how could she say the Shemang either?

Having heard the verdict of the doctor, Ali returned in hot haste, and silenced both the bond-women. The Imám was a villain, and the Chacham was a thief; there was only one good man left in Tetuan, and that was his own Táleb, his school-master, the same that had taught him the harp in the days of the Governor's marriage. This person was an old negro, bewrinkled by years, becrippled by ague, once stone deaf, and still partially so, half blind, and reputed to be only half wise, a liberated slave from the Sahara, just able to read the Koran and the Torah, and willing to teach either impartially, according to his knowledge, for he was neither a Jew

nor a Muslim, but a little of both, as he used to say,
and not too much of either. For such a hybrid in a
land of intolerance there must have been no place
save the dungeons of the Kasbah, but that this good
nondescript was a privileged pet of everybody. In
his dark cellar, down an alley by the side of the
Grand Mosque in the Metámar, he had sat from
early morning until sunset year in, year out, through
thirty years, on his rush-covered floor, among
successive generations of his boys, and as often as
night fell he had gone hither and thither among the
sick and dying, carrying comfort of kind words, and
often meat and drink of his meagre substance.

Such was Ali's hero after Israel, and now in
Israel's absence and his own great trouble, he hied
away for him.

" Father," cried the lad, " does it not say in the
good book that the prayer of a righteous man
availeth much ? "

" It does, my son," said the Táleb. " You have
truth. What then ? "

"Then if you will pray for Naomi she will recover," said Ali.

It was a sweet instance of simple faith. The old black Táleb dismissed his scholars, closed down his shutter, locked it with a padlock, hobbled to Naomi's bedside in his tattered white selham, looked down at her through the big spectacles that sprawled over his broad black nose, and then, while a dim mist floated between the spectacles and his eyes, and a great lump rose at his throat to choke him, he fell to the floor and prayed, and Ali and the black women knelt beside him.

The negro's prayer was simple to childishness. It told God everything; it recited the facts to the heavenly Father as to one who was far away and might not know. The maiden was sick unto death. She had been three days and nights knowing no one, and eating and drinking nothing. She was blind and dumb and deaf. Her father loved her and was wrapped up in her. She was his only child, and his wife was dead, and he was a lonely man. He was away from his home now, and if, when he returned, the girl were gone and lost—if she were dead and buried—his strong heart would be broken and his very soul in peril.

It was a touching spectacle—the dumb angel of white and crimson turning and tossing on the bed in an aureole of her streaming yellow hair, and the four black faces about her, eager and hot and aflame, with closed eyelids and open lips, calling down mercy out of heaven from the God that might be seen by the soul alone.

And so it was, but whether by chance or Providence let no man dare to tell, that even while the four black people were yet on their knees by the bed, the turning and tossing of the white face stopped suddenly, and Naomi lay still on her pillow. The hot flush faded from her cheeks; her features, which had twitched, were quiet; and her hands, which had been restless, lay at peace on the counterpane.

The good old Táleb took this for an answer to his prayer, and he shouted " El hamdu l'Illah ! " (Praise

be to God), while the big drops coursed down the
deep furrows of his steaming face. And then, as if
to complete the miracle, and to establish the old
man's faith in it, a strange and wondrous thing befell.
First, a thin watery humour flowed from one of
Naomi's ears, and after that she raised herself on her
elbow. Her eyes were open as if they saw; her lips
were parted as though they were breaking into a
smile; she made a long sigh like one who has slept
softly through the night and has just awakened in
the morning.

Then, while the black people held their breath in
their first moment of surprise and gladness, her
parted lips gave forth a sound. It was a laugh—a
faint, broken, bankrupt echo of her old happy
laughter. And then instantly, almost before the
others had heard the sound, and while the notes of
it were yet coming from her tongue, she lifted her
idle hand and covered her ear, and over her face there
passed a look of dread.

So swift had this change been that the bondwomen

had not seen it, and they were shouting " Hallelujah "
with one voice, thinking only that she who had been
dead to them was alive again. But the old Táleb
cried eagerly, "Hush! my children, hush! What
is coming is a marvellous thing! I know what it is
—who knows so well as I? Once I was deaf, my
children, but now I hear. Listen! The maiden has
had fever—fever of the brain. Listen! A watery
humour had gathered in her head. It has gone; it
has flowed away. Now she will hear. Listen, for it
is I that know it—who knows it so well as I? Yes ;
she will be no longer deaf. Her ears will be opened.
She will hear. Once she was living in a land of
silence; now she is coming into the land of sound.
Blessed be God, for He has wrought this wondrous
work. God is great! God is mighty! Praise the
merciful God for ever! El hamdu l'Illah ! "

And strange and marvellous and passing belief as
the old Táleb's story seemed to be, it appeared to be
coming to pass, for even while he spoke, beginning
in a slow whisper and going on with quicker and

louder breath, Naomi turned her face full upon him; and when the black women, in their ready faith, joined in his shouts of praise, she turned her face towards them also; and wheresoever a voice was made in the room she inclined her head towards it anxiously as one who heard, and also as one who was in fear of the sounds that assailed her.

But, seeing nothing of her look of pain, and knowing nothing but one thing only, and that was the wondrous and mighty change that she who had been deaf could now hear, that she who had never before heard speech now heard their voices as they spoke around her, Ali, in his frantic delight, laughing and crying together, his white teeth aglitter, and his round black face shining with tears, began to shout and to sing, and to dance around the bed in wild joy at the miracle which God had wrought in answer to his old Táleb's prayer. No heed did he pay to the Táleb's cries of warning, but danced on and on, and neither did the bondwomen see the old man's uplifted arms or his big lips pursed out in hushes, so over-

powered were they with their delight, so startled and
so joy-drunken. But over their tumult there came
a wild outburst of piercing shrieks. They were the
cries of Naomi in her blind and sudden terror at the
first sound that had reached her of human voices.
Her face was blanched, her eyelids were trembling,
her lips were restless, her nostrils quivered, her whole
being seemed to be overcome by a vertigo of dread,
and, in the horrible disarray of all her sensations, her
brain, on its awakening from its dolorous sleep of
three delirious days, was tottering and reeling at its
welcome in this world of noise.

Then Ali ended suddenly his frantic dance, the
bondwomen held their peace in an instant, and blank
silence in the chamber followed the clamour of tongues.

It was at this great moment that Israel, returning
from his journey in the jellab of a Moor, knocked like
a stranger at his outer door. When he entered the
chamber, still clad as a torn and ragged man, too
eager to remove the sorry garments which had been
given to him on the way, Naomi was resting against

the pillar of the bed. He saw that her countenance was changed, and that every feature of her face seemed to listen. No longer was it as the face of a lamb that is simple and content, neither was it as the face of a child that is peaceful and happy; but it was hot, and perplexed. Fear sat on her face, and wonder and questioning; and as Fatimah stood by her side, speaking tender words to comfort her, no cheer did she seem to get from them, but only dread, for she drew away from her when she spoke, as though the sound of the voice smote her ears with terror of trouble. All this Israel saw on the instant, and then his sight grew dim, his heart beat as if it would kill him, a thick mist seemed to cover every-thing, and through the dense waves of semi-conscious-ness he heard the dull hum of Fatimah's muffled voice coming to him as from far away.

"My pretty Naomi! My little heart! My sweet jewel of gold and silver! It is nothing! Nothing! Look! See! Her father has come back! Her dear father has come back to her!"

Presently the room ceased to go round and round, and Israel knew that Naomi's arms surrounded him, that his own arms enlaced her, and that her head was pressed hard against his bosom. Yes, it was she! It was Naomi! Ali had told him truth. She lived! She was well! She had ears to hear! The old hope that had chirped in his soul was justified, and the dear delicious dream was come true. Oh! God was great, God was good, God had given him more than he had asked or deserved!

Thus for some minutes he stood motionless, blessing the God of Jacob, yet uttering no words, for his heart was too full for speech, only holding Naomi closely to him, while his tears fell on her blind face. And the black people in the chamber wept to see it, that not more dumb in that great hour of gladness was she who was born so than he to whose house had come the wonderful work that God had wrought.

No heed had Israel given yet to the bodeful signs in Naomi's face, in joy over such as were joyful. When he had taken her in his arms she had known him, and she had clung to him in her glad surprise. But when she continued to lie on his bosom it was not only because he was her father and she loved him, and because he had been lost to her and was found. It was also because he alone was silent of all them that were about her.

When he saw this his heart was humbled, but he understood her fears, that coming out of a land of great silence, where the voice of man was never heard, where the air was songless as the air of dreams and darkling as the air of a tomb, her soul misgave her, and her spirit trembled in a new world of strange sounds. For what was the ear but a little dark chamber, a vault, a dungeon in a castle, wherein the soul was ever passing to and fro, asking for news of the world without? Through seventeen dark and silent years the soul of Naomi had been passing and repassing within its beautiful tabernacle of flesh, crying daily and hourly, " Watchman, what of the world ? " At length it had found an answer, and it was terrified. The world had spoken to her soul, and its voice was like the reverberations of a subterranean cavern, strange and deep and awful.

In that first moment of Israel's consciousness after he entered the room, all four black folks seemed to be speaking together.

Ali was saying, " Father, those dogs and thieves of tentmen and muleteers returned yesterday, and said—— "

And the bondwomen were crying, " Sidi, you were right when you went away ! " " Yes, the dear child was ill ! " " Oh, how she missed you when you were gone ! " " She has been delirious, and the doctor, the son of Tetuan—— "

And the old Táleb was muttering, " Master, it is all by God's mercy. We prayed for the life of the maiden, and lo ! He has given us this gateway to her spirit as well."

Then Israel saw that as their voices entered the dark vault of Naomi's ears they startled and distressed her. So, to pacify her, he motioned them out of the chamber. They went away without a word.

The reason of Naomi's fears began to dawn upon them. An awe seemed to be cast over her by the solemnity of that great moment. It was like to the birth-moment of a soul.

And when the black people were gone from the room, Israel closed the door of it that he might shut out the noises of the streets, for women were calling to their children without, and the children were still shouting in their play. This being done, he returned to Naomi and rested her head against his bosom and soothed her with his hand, and she put her arms about his neck and clung to him. And while he did so his heart yearned to speak to her, and to see by her face that she could hear. Let it be but one word, only one, that she might know her father's voice—for she had never once heard it—and answer it with a smile.

" Daughter ! My dearest ! My darling ! "

Only this, nothing more ! Only one sweet word of all the unspoken tenderness which, like a river without any outlet, had been seventeen years dammed

up in his breast. But no, it could not be. He must
not speak lest her face should frown and her arms be
drawn away. To see that would break his heart.
Nevertheless, he wrestled with the temptation. It
was terrible. He dared not risk it. So he sat on
the bed in silence, hardly moving, scarcely breathing
—a dust-laden man in a ragged jellab, holding
Naomi in his arms.

It was still the month of Ramadhán, and the sun
was but three hours set. In the fondak called El Nsaá,
a group of the town Moors, who had fasted through
the day, were feasting and carousing. Over the walls
of the Mellah, from the direction of the Spanish inn
at the entrance to the little tortuous quarter of the
shoemakers, there came at intervals a hubbub of
voices, and occasionally wild shouts and cries. The
day was Wednesday, the market-day of Tetuan, and
on the open space called the Feddán many fires were
lighted at the mouths of tents, and men and women and
children—country Arabs and Berbers—were squatting around the charcoal embers, eating and drinking

and talking and laughing, while the ruddy glow lit
up their swarthy faces in the darkness. But presently the wing of night fell over both Moorish town
and Mellah ; the traffic of the streets came to an end ;
the " Bálak " of the ass-driver was no more heard, the
slipper of the Jew sounded but rarely on the pavement, the fires on the Feddán died out, the hubbub
of the fondak and the wild shouts of the shoemakers'
quarter were hushed, and quieter and more quiet
grew the air until all was still.

At the coming of peace Naomi's fears seemed to
abate. Her clinging arms released their hold of her
father's neck, and with a trembling sigh she dropped
back on to the pillow. And in this hour of stillness
she would have slept; but even while Israel was
lifting up his heart in thankfulness to God that He
was making the way of her great journey easy out of
the land of silence into the land of speech a storm
broke over the town. Through many hot days preceding it had been gathering in the air, which had
the echoing hollowness of a vault. It was loud and

long and terrible. First, from the direction of
Marteel, over the four miles which divide Tetuan
from the coast, came the warning which the sea sends
before trouble comes to the land—a deep moan as of
waters falling from the sky. Next came the moan
of the wind down the valley that opens on the gate
called the Bab el Marsa, and along the river that
flows to the port. Then came the roll of thunder,
like a million cannon, down the gorges of the Reef
mountains and across the plain that stretches far
away to Kitán. Last of all, the black clouds of the
sky emptied themselves over the town, and the rain
fell in floods on the roof of the house and on the
pavement of the patio, and leapt up again in great
loud drops, making a noise to the ear like to the
tramp, tramp, tramp of a hidden multitude. Thus
sound after sound broke over the darkness of the
night in a thousand awful voices, now near, now far,
now loud, now low, now long, now short, now rising,
now falling, now rushing, now running—a mighty
tumult and a fearsome anarchy.

At this Naomi's terror was redoubled. Every sound seemed to smite her body as a blow. Hitherto she had known one sense only, the sense of touch, and though now she knew the sense of hearing also, she continued to refer all sensations to feeling. At the sound of the sea she put out her arms before her; at the sound of the wind she buried her face in her palms; and at the sound of the thunder she lifted her hands as if to protect her head.

Meanwhile, Israel sat beside her and cherished her close at his bosom. He yearned to speak words of comfort to her, soft words of cheer, tender words of love, gentle words of hope.

" Be not afraid, my daughter ! It is only the wind, it is only the rain ; it is only the thunder. Once you loved to run and race in them. They shall not harm you, for God is good and He will keep you safe. There, there, my little heart! See, your father is with you. He will guard you. Fear not, my child, fear not ! "

Such were the words which Israel yearned to speak

in Naomi's ears, but, alas! what words could she understand any more than the wind which moaned about the house and the thunder which rolled overhead? And again and again, alas! as surely as he spoke to her she must shrink from the solace of his voice even as she shrank from the tumult of the voices of the storm.

Israel fell back helpless and heartbroken. He began to see in its fulness the change which had befallen Naomi, yet not at once to realise it, so sudden and so numbing was the stroke. He began to know that with the mighty blessing for which he had hoped and prayed—the blessing of a pathway to his daughter's soul—a misfortune had come as well. What was it to him now that Naomi had ears to hear if she could not understand? And what was this tempest to the maiden new-born out of the land of silence into the world of sound, yet still both blind and dumb, but a circle of darkness alive with creatures that groaned and cried and shrieked and moved around her?

Thus nothing could Israel do but watch the creeping of Naomi's terror, and smooth her forehead and chafe her hands. And this he did, until at length, in a fresh outbreak of the storm, when the vault of the heavens seemed rent asunder, a strong delirium took hold of her, and she fell to a long unconsciousness. Then Israel held back his heart no longer, but wept above her, and called to her, and cried aloud upon her name:

"Naomi! Naomi! My poor child! My dearest! Hear me! It is nothing! nothing! Listen! It is gone! Gone!"

With such passionate cries of love and sorrow Israel gave vent to his soul in its trouble. And while Naomi lay in her unconsciousness, he knew not what feelings possessed him, for his heart was in a great turmoil. Desolate! desolate! All was desolate! His high-built hopes were in ashes!

Sometimes he remembered the days when the child knew not sorrow, and grief came not near her, when she was brighter than the sun which she could not see and sweeter than the songs which she could not hear, when she was joyous as a bird in its narrow cage and fretted not at the bars which bound her, when she laughed as she braided her hair and came dancing out of her chamber at dawn. And, remembering this, he looked down at her knitted face, and his heart grew bitter, and he lifted up his voice through the tumult of the storm, and cried again on the God of Jacob, and rebuked Him for the marvellous work which He had wrought.

If God were an almighty God, surely He looked before and after, and foresaw what must come to pass. And, foreseeing and knowing all, why had God answered his prayer? He himself had been a fool. Why had he craved God's pity? Once his poor child was blither than the panther of the wilderness and happier than the young lamb that sports in springtime. If she was blind, she knew not what it was to see; and if she was deaf, she knew not what it was to hear; and if she was dumb, she knew not what it was to speak. Nothing did she miss of sight or sound or speech any more than of the wings of the eagle or the dove. Yet he would not be content; he would not be appeased. Oh! subtlety of the devil which had brought this evil upon him!

But the God whom Israel in his agony and his madness rebuked in this manner sent His angel to make a great silence, and the storm lapsed to a breathless quiet.

And when the tempest was gone Naomi's delirium passed away. She seemed to look, and nothing could she see; and then to listen, and nothing could she hear; and then she clasped the hand of her father that lay over her hand, and sighed and sank down again.

"Ah!"

It was even as if peace had come to her with the thought that she was back in the land of great silence once again, and that the voices which had startled her, and the storm which had terrified her, had been nothing but an evil dream.

In that sweet respite she fell asleep, and Israel

forgot the reproaches with which he had reproached his God, and looked tenderly down at her, and said within himself: "It was her baptism. Now she will walk the world with confidence, and never again will she be afraid. Truly the Lord our God is king over all kingdoms and wise beyond all wisdom!"

Then, with one look backward at Naomi where she slept, he crept out of the room on tiptoe.

END OF VOL. I.

PRINTED BY BALLANTYNE, HANSON AND CO.
LONDON AND EDINBURGH.

Telegraphic Address—
Sunlocks, London.

June 1891.

Mr. William Heinemann's

Announcements

AND

New Publications.

Now Ready.

IMPERIAL GERMANY.

A CRITICAL STUDY OF FACT AND CHARACTER.

By SIDNEY WHITMAN.

NEW EDITION, REVISED AND ENLARGED.

Small crown 8vo, cloth, 3s. 6d. ; paper, 2s. 6d.

OPINIONS ON "IMPERIAL GERMANY."

Count Moltke.—"I have read this study on Germany with the greatest interest. There can be no doubt that every State requires a government suited to its individual idiosyncrasies. A Constitution like that of England—secure through her geographical position—a Constitution gradually developed out of the character of the nation, could never be transferred to the continent of Europe.

"France—during the last century—has tried alternately monarchy in various forms, empire, and republic, without arriving at any definite result.

"Germany, on the other hand, only so recently united as an Empire, is an intruder, a *parvenu*, in the family of European States. Hemmed in between mighty neighbours, we are of opinion that we require a strong monarchy. It was therefore a great pleasure for me to find that full justice had been done to the ancient and proven paternal government of the Hohenzollern."

Prince Bismarck.—"I consider the different chapters of this book masterly."

Professor Blackie.—"I class this work with Aristotle's Politics and Bryce's America, as one of the three best books on the concrete philosophy of politics that I know. No better work could be placed into the hands of our modern false prophets of liberty and irreverence than the chapters on the Prussian Monarchy. And yet, though the author's main business is to exhibit excellence, he is always just, and never attempts to veil the faults or to deny the dangers that belong to any form of social organisation."

Professor Goldwin Smith.—"I hope it is not presumptuous in a stranger to express to you the pleasure with which he has read your 'Imperial Germany,' especially that part of it in which you do justice to Bismarck."

Now Ready.

In Two Volumes, Demy 8vo, with Portraits, 30s. net.

DE QUINCEY MEMORIALS.

BEING LETTERS AND OTHER RECORDS HERE FIRST PUB-
LISHED, WITH COMMUNICATIONS FROM COLERIDGE, THE
WORDSWORTHS, HANNAH MORE, PROFESSOR WILSON,
AND OTHERS.

Edited, with Introduction, Notes, and Narrative,

By ALEXANDER H. JAPP, LL.D., F.R.S.E.

Daily Telegraph.—"Few works of greater literary interest have of late years issued from the press than the two volumes of 'De Quincey Memorials.' They comprise most valuable materials for the historian of literary and social England at the beginning of the century; but they are not on that account less calculated to amuse, enlighten, and absorb the general reader of biographical memoirs."

POSTHUMOUS WORKS OF THOMAS DE QUINCEY.

VOLUME I. Crown 8vo, 6s.

SUSPIRIA DE PROFUNDIS.

WITH OTHER ESSAYS,
CRITICAL, HISTORICAL, BIOGRAPHICAL, PHILOSOPHICAL,
IMAGINATIVE, AND HUMOROUS.

Edited, with Introduction and Notes, from the Author's Original MSS., by

ALEXANDER H. JAPP, LL.D., F.R.S.E., &c.

The Times.—"Here we have De Quincey at his best. Will be welcome to lovers of De Quincey and lovers of good literature."

Anti-Jacobin.—"In these Suspiria De Quincey writes with the sonorous grandeur of Cicero, while his subject is some vision or imagination worthy of Poe."

21 BEDFORD STREET, LONDON, W.C.   3

Now Ready.

In One Volume, Crown 8vo, 3s. 6d.

PRETTY MISS SMITH.

A NOVEL.

By FLORENCE WARDEN.

Author of "The House on the Marsh," "A Witch of the Hills," &c.

Punch.—"Since Miss Florence Warden's 'House on the Marsh,'" says the Baron, "I have not read a more exciting tale than the authoress's 'Pretty Miss Smith.' It should be swallowed right off at a sitting."

In One Volume, Crown 8vo, 3s. 6d.

A ROMANCE OF THE CAPE FRONTIER.

By BERTRAM MITFORD.

Author of "Through the Zulu Country," &c.

Academy.—"The love story is a particularly pleasing one.

One Volume, Crown 8vo, 3s. 6d.

LOS CERRITOS.

A ROMANCE OF THE MODERN TIME.

By GERTRUDE FRANKLIN ATHERTON.

Author of "Hermia Suydam," and "What Dreams may Come."

Athenæum.—"Full of fresh fancies and suggestions. Told with strength and delicacy. A decidedly charming romance."

One Volume, Crown 8vo, 3s. 6d.

A MODERN MARRIAGE.

A NOVEL.

By THE MARQUISE CLARA LANZA.

Queen.—"A powerful story, dramatically and consistently carried out."

Black and White.—"A decidedly clever book."

HEINEMANN'S INTERNATIONAL LIBRARY.

EDITED BY EDMUND GOSSE.

˙.˙ Each Volume has an Introduction specially written by the Editor.

IN GOD'S WAY. By BJÖRNSTJERNE BJÖRNSON.

Translated from the Norwegian by ELIZABETH CAR-MICHAEL. In One Volume, crown 8vo, 3s. 6d. ; or Paper Covers, 2s. 6d.

Athenæum.—"Without doubt the most important, and the most interesting work published during the twelve months. . . . There are descriptions which certainly belong to the best and cleverest things our literature has ever produced. Amongst the many characters, the doctor's wife is unquestionably the first. It would be difficult to find anything more tender, soft, and refined than this charming personage."

Saturday Review.—"The English reader could desire no better introduction to contemporary foreign fiction than this notable novel.

Speaker.—"'In God's Way' is really a notable book."

PIERRE AND JEAN. By GUY DE MAUPASSANT.

Translated from the French by CLARA BELL. In One Volume, crown 8vo, 3s. 6d. ; or Paper Covers, 2s. 6d.

Pall Mall Gazette.—"So fine and faultless, so perfectly balanced, so steadily progressive, so clear and simple and satisfying. It is admirable from beginning to end."

Athenæum.—"Ranks amongst the best gems of modern French fiction."

THE CHIEF JUSTICE. By KARL EMIL FRANZOS.

Author of "For the Right," &c. Translated from the German by MILES CORBET. One Volume, crown 8vo, 3s. 6d. ; or Paper Covers, 2s. 6d.

The New Review.—"Few novels of recent times have a more sustained and vivid human interest."

Christian World.—A story of wonderful power . . . as free from anything objectionable as 'The Heart of Midlothian.'"

Manchester Guardian.—"Simple, forcible, and intensely tragic. It is a very powerful study, singularly grand in its simplicity."

Sunday Times.—"A series of dramatic scenes welded together with a never-failing interest and skill."

HEINEMANN'S INTERNATIONAL LIBRARY—*(continued)*.

WORK WHILE YE HAVE THE LIGHT. By
COUNT LYOF TOLSTOI. Translated from the Russian by
E. J. DILLON, Ph.D. In One Volume, crown 8vo, 3s. 6d.;
or Paper Covers, 2s. 6d.

Glasgow Herald.—"Mr. Gosse gives a brief biographical sketch of
Tolstoi, and an interesting estimate of his literary productions."
Scotsman.—"It is impossible to convey any adequate idea of the
simplicity and force with which the work is unfolded ; no one who
reads the book will dispute its author's greatness."
Liverpool Mercury.—"Marked by all the old power of the great
Russian novelist."
Manchester Guardian.—"Readable and well translated; full of
high and noble feeling."

FANTASY. By MATILDE SERAO. Translated from
the Italian by HENRY HARLAND and PAUL SYLVESTER.
In One Volume, crown 8vo, 3s. 6d. ; or Paper Covers,
2s. 6d.

National Observer.—"The strongest work from the hand of a
woman that has been published for many a day."
Scottish Leader.—"The book is full of a glowing and living
realism. . . . There is nothing like 'Fantasy' in modern literature.
. . . It is a work of elfish art, a mosaic of life and love, of right and
wrong, of human weakness and strength, and purity and wantonness,
pieced together in deft and witching precision."

FROTH. By DON ARMANDO PALACIO VALDÉS.
Translated from the Spanish by CLARA BELL. In One
Volume, crown 8vo, 3s. 6d. ; or Paper Covers, 2s. 6d.

Daily Telegraph.—"Vigorous and powerful in the highest degree.
It abounds in forcible delineation of character, and describes scenes
with rare and graphic strength."

In the Press.

THE COMMODORE'S DAUGHTERS. By JONAS
LIE. Translated from the Norwegian by H. L. BRÆK-
STAD and GERTRUDE HUGHES.

FOOTSTEPS OF FATE. By LOUIS COUPERUS.
Translated from the Dutch by CLARA BELL.

HEINEMANN'S SCIENTIFIC HANDBOOKS.

Now Ready.

In One Volume, Crown 8vo, Illustrated, 7s. 6d.

MANUAL OF ASSAYING GOLD, SILVER, COPPER, AND LEAD ORES.

By WALTER LEE BROWN, B.Sc.

REVISED, CORRECTED, AND CONSIDERABLY ENLARGED,

WITH A CHAPTER ON THE ASSAYING OF FUEL, ETC.

By A. B. GRIFFITHS, Ph.D., F.R.S. (Edin.), F.C.S.

Colliery Guardian.—"A delightful and fascinating book."

Financial World.—"The most complete and practical manual on everything which concerns assaying of all which have come before us."

North British Economist.—"With this book the amateur may become an expert. Bankers and Bullion Brokers are equally likely to find it useful."

In One Volume, Crown 8vo, Illustrated, 5s.

THE PHYSICAL PROPERTIES OF GASES.

By ARTHUR L. KIMBALL,

OF THE JOHNS HOPKINS UNIVERSITY.

Chemical News.—"The man of culture who wishes for a general and accurate acquaintance with the physical properties of gases, will find in Mr. Kimball's work just what he requires."

Iron.—"We can highly recommend this little book."

Manchester Guardian.—"Mr. Kimball has the too rare merit of describing first the facts, and then the hypotheses invented to limn them together."

In One Volume, Crown 8vo, Illustrated, 5s.

HEAT AS A FORM OF ENERGY.

By PROFESSOR R. H. THURSTON,

OF CORNELL UNIVERSITY.

Manchester Examiner.—"Bears out the character of its predecessors for careful and correct statement and deduction under the light of the most recent discoveries."

Scotsman.—"A popular account of what science has to say of heat as a form of energy. There is not a more interesting chapter in all science, and the book has solid qualities enough to recommend it widely."

HEINEMANN'S INTERNATIONAL LIBRARY.

EDITED BY EDMUND GOSSE.

. Each Volume has an Introduction specially written by
the Editor.

IN GOD'S WAY. By BJÖRNSTJERNE BJÖRNSON.

Translated from the Norwegian by ELIZABETH CAR-
MICHAEL. In One Volume, crown 8vo, 3s. 6d. ; or Paper
Covers, 2s. 6d.

Athenæum.—"Without doubt the most important, and the most
interesting work published during the twelve months. . . . There are
descriptions which certainly belong to the best and cleverest things
our literature has ever produced. Amongst the many characters, the
doctor's wife is unquestionably the first. It would be difficult to find
anything more tender, soft, and refined than this charming personage."

Saturday Review.—"The English reader could desire no better
introduction to contemporary foreign fiction than this notable novel.

Speaker.—"'In God's Way' is really a notable book."

PIERRE AND JEAN. By GUY DE MAUPASSANT.

Translated from the French by CLARA BELL. In One
Volume, crown 8vo, 3s. 6d. ; or Paper Covers, 2s. 6d.

Pall Mall Gazette.—"So fine and faultless, so perfectly balanced,
so steadily progressive, so clear and simple and satisfying. It is
admirable from beginning to end."

Athenæum.—"Ranks amongst the best gems of modern French
fiction."

THE CHIEF JUSTICE. By KARL EMIL FRANZOS.

Author of "For the Right," &c. Translated from the
German by MILES CORBET. One Volume, crown 8vo,
3s. 6l. ; or Paper Covers, 2s. 6d.

The New Review.—"Few novels of recent times have a more
sustained and vivid human interest."

Christian World.—A story of wonderful power . . . as free from
anything objectionable as 'The Heart of Midlothian.'"

Manchester Guardian.—"Simple, forcible, and intensely tragic.
It is a very powerful study, singularly grand in its simplicity."

Sunday Times.—"A series of dramatic scenes welded together
with a never-failing interest and skill."

HEINEMANN'S INTERNATIONAL LIBRARY—(*continued*).

WORK WHILE YE HAVE THE LIGHT. By
Count Lyof Tolstoi. Translated from the Russian by E. J. Dillon, Ph.D. In One Volume, crown 8vo, 3s. 6d.; or Paper Covers, 2s. 6d.

Glasgow Herald.—"Mr. Gosse gives a brief biographical sketch of Tolstoi, and an interesting estimate of his literary productions."
Scotsman.—"It is impossible to convey any adequate idea of the simplicity and force with which the work is unfolded ; no one who reads the book will dispute its author's greatness."
Liverpool Mercury.—"Marked by all the old power of the great Russian novelist."
Manchester Guardian.—"Readable and well translated ; full of high and noble feeling."

FANTASY. By Matilde Serao. Translated from
the Italian by Henry Harland and Paul Sylvester. In One Volume, crown 8vo, 3s. 6d. ; or Paper Covers, 2s. 6d.

National Observer.—"The strongest work from the hand of a woman that has been published for many a day."
Scottish Leader.—"The book is full of a glowing and living realism. . . . There is nothing like 'Fantasy' in modern literature. . . . It is a work of elfish art, a mosaic of life and love, of right and wrong, of human weakness and strength, and purity and wantonness, pieced together in deft and witching precision."

FROTH. By Don Armando Palacio Valdés.
Translated from the Spanish by Clara Bell. In One Volume, crown 8vo, 3s. 6d. ; or Paper Covers, 2s. 6d.

Daily Telegraph.—"Vigorous and powerful in the highest degree. It abounds in forcible delineation of character, and describes scenes with rare and graphic strength."

In the Press.

THE COMMODORE'S DAUGHTERS. By Jonas
Lie. Translated from the Norwegian by H. L. Brækstad and Gertrude Hughes.

FOOTSTEPS OF FATE. By Louis Couperus.
Translated from the Dutch by Clara Bell.

New Works of Fiction.

THE BONDMAN. A New Saga. By HALL

CAINE. Fourth Edition (Sixteenth Thousand). In One
Volume. Crown 8vo, 3s. 6d.

Mr. Gladstone.—"The 'Bondman' is a work of which I recognise
the freshness, vigour, and sustained interest no less than its integrity
of aim."

Count Tolstoi.—"A book I have read with deep interest."

Standard.—"Its argument is grand, and it is sustained with a
power that is almost marvellous."

IN THE VALLEY. A Novel. By HAROLD

FREDERIC, Author of "The Lawton Girl," "Seth's
Brother's Wife," &c. &c. In Three Volumes. Crown
8vo, with Illustrations.

Mr. Gladstone.—"It has a great historical interest from its
apparently faithful exhibition of the relations of the different nation-
alities and races who were so curiously grouped together in and about
the State of New York, before the war of American independence."

Athenæum.—"A romantic story, both graphic and exciting, not
merely in the central picture itself, but also in its weird surroundings.
This is a novel deserving to be read."

Manchester Examiner.—"Certain to win the reader's admiration.
'In the Valley' is a novel that deserves to live."

Scotsman.—"A work of real ability; it stands apart from the
common crowd of three-volume novels."

A MARKED MAN: Some Episodes in his

Life. By ADA CAMBRIDGE, Author of "Two Years'
Time," "A Mere Chance," &c. &c. In Three Volumes,
crown 8vo.

Morning Post.—"A depth of feeling, a knowledge of the human
heart, and an amount of tact that one rarely finds. Should take a
prominent place among the novels of the season."

Illustrated London News.—"The moral tone of this story, rightly
considered, is pure and noble, though it deals with the problem of
an unhappy marriage."

Pall Mall Gazette.—"Contains one of the best written stories of a
mésalliance that is to be found in modern fiction."

ꩍew ꟿꪮrꪰs of ꟾiction.

THE MOMENT AFTER: A Tale of the Unseen. By ROBERT BUCHANAN. Popular Edition, crown 8vo, 1s.

Athenæum.—"Should be read—in daylight."

Observer.—"A clever *tour de force*."

Guardian.—"Particularly impressive, graphic, and powerful."

Bristol Mercury.—"Written with the same poetic feeling and power which have given a rare charm to Mr. Buchanan's previous prose writings."

COME FORTH! By ELIZABETH STUART PHELPS and HERBERT D. WARD. In One Volume, imperial 16mo, 7s. 6d.

Scotsman.—"'Come Forth!' is the story of the raising of Lazarus, amplified into a dramatic love-story. . . . It has a simple, forthright dramatic interest such as is seldom attained except in purely imaginative fiction."

THE MASTER OF THE MAGICIANS. By ELIZABETH STUART PHELPS and HERBERT D. WARD. In One Volume, imperial 16mo, 7s. 6d.

The Athenæum.—"A success in Biblical fiction."

THE DOMINANT SEVENTH: A Musical Story. By KATE ELIZABETH CLARK. In One Volume, crown 8vo, 5s.

Speaker.—"A very romantic story."

A VERY STRANGE FAMILY; A Novel. By F. W. ROBINSON, Author of "Grandmother's Money," "Lazarus in London," &c. &c. In One Volume, crown 8vo, 3s. 6d.

Glasgow Herald.—"An ingeniously-devised plot, of which the interest is kept up to the very last page. A judicious blending of humour and pathos further helps to make the book delightful reading from start to finish."

New Works of Fiction.

HAUNTINGS: Fantastic Stories. By VERNON

LEE, Author of "Baldwin," "Miss Brown," &c. &c. In One Volume, crown 8vo, 6s.

Pall Mall Gazette.—"Well imagined, cleverly constructed, powerfully executed. 'Dionea' is a fine and impressive idea, and 'Oke of Okehurst' a masterly story."

PASSION THE PLAYTHING. A Novel. By

R. MURRAY GILCHRIST. In One Volume, crown 8vo, 6s.

Athenæum.—"This well-written story must be read to be appreciated."

Yorkshire Post.—"A book to lay hold of the reader."

Recent Publications.

THE LABOUR MOVEMENT IN AMERICA.

By RICHARD T. ELY, Ph.D., Associate in Political Economy, Johns Hopkins University. In One Volume, crown 8vo, 5s.

Weekly Despatch.—"There is much to interest and instruct."
Saturday Review.—"Both interesting and valuable."
England.—"Full of information and thought."
National Reformer.—"Chapter iii. deals with the growth and present condition of labour organisations in America . . . this forms a most valuable page of history."

ARABIC AUTHORS: A Manual of Arabian

History and Literature. By F. F. ARBUTHNOT, M.R.A.S., Author of "Early Ideas," "Persian Portraits," &c. In One Volume, 8vo, 10s.

Manchester Examiner.—"The whole work has been carefully indexed, and will prove a handbook of the highest value to the student who wishes to gain a better acquaintance with Arabian letters."

Recent Publications.

THE GENTLE ART OF MAKING EN

As pleasingly exemplified in many instances, the serious ones of this earth, carefully exasperated, have been prettily spurred on to indiscretions and unseemliness, while overcome by an undue sense of right. By J. M'NEIL WHISTLER. In One Volume, pott 4to, 10s. 6d.

Punch, *June 21.*—"The book in itself, in its binding, print, and arrangement, is a work of art."

Punch, *June 28.*—"A work of rare humour, a thing of beauty and a joy for now and ever."

THE PASSION PLAY AT OBERAMMERGAU,

1890. By F. W. FARRAR, D.D., F.R.S., Archdeacon and Canon of Westminster, &c. &c. In One Volume, small 4to, 2s. 6d.

Spectator.—"Among the many accounts that have been written this year of 'The Passion Play,' one of the most picturesque, the most interesting, and the most reasonable, is this sketch of Archdeacon Farrar's. . . . This little book will be read with delight by those who have, and by those who have not, visited Oberammergau."

THE GARDEN'S STORY; or, Pleasures and

Trials of an Amateur Gardener. By G. H. ELL-WANGER. With an Introduction by the Rev. C. WOLLEY DOD. In One Volume, 12mo, with Illustrations, 5s.

Scotsman.—"Deserves every recommendation that a pleasant-looking page can give it; for it deals with a charming subject in a charming manner. Mr. Ellwanger talks delightfully, with instruction but without pedantry, of the flowers, the insects, and the birds. . . . It will give pleasure to every reader who takes the smallest interest in flowers, and ought to find many readers."

THE LIFE OF HENRIK IBSEN. By HENRIK

JÆGER. Translated by CLARA BELL. With the Verse done into English from the Norwegian Original by EDMUND GOSSE. In One Volume, crown 8vo, 6s.

St. James's Gazette.—"Admirably translated. Deserves a cordial and emphatic welcome."

Guardian.—"Ibsen's dramas at present enjoy a considerable vogue, and their admirers will rejoice to find full descriptions and criticisms in Mr. Jæger's book."

Academy.—"We welcome it heartily. An unqualified boon to the many English students of Ibsen."

COMMUNICATIONS ON A REMEDY FOR

TUBERCULOSIS. By Professor ROBERT KOCH, Berlin. Authorised Translation. 8vo, Wrapper, 1s. ; or Limp Cloth, 1s. 6d.

From The Times, leading article, November 17, 1890:—"It has been acknowledged, at any time during the last year or two, that the discovery of a cure for tuberculosis was not only possible but even likely ; and that which is now announced comes with the highest recommendations and from the most trustworthy source."

IDLE MUSINGS: Essays in Social Mosaic.

By E. CONDER GRAY, Author of "Wise Words and Loving Deeds," &c. &c. In One Volume, crown 8vo, 6s.

Saturday Review.—"Light, brief, and bright are the 'essays in social mosaic.' Mr. Gray ranges like a butterfly from high themes to trivial with a good deal of dexterity and a profusion of illustrations."

Graphic.—"Pleasantly written, will serve admirably to wile away an idle half-hour or two."

IVY AND PASSION FLOWER: Poems. By

GERARD BENDALL, Author of "Estelle," &c. &c. 12mo, 3s. 6d.

Scotsman.—"Will be read with pleasure."

Woman.—"There is a delicacy of touch and simplicity about the poems which is very attractive."

Musical World.—"The poems are delicate specimens of art, graceful and polished."

VERSES. By GERTRUDE HALL. 12mo, 3s. 6d.

Musical World.—"Interesting volume of verse."

Woman.—"Very sweet and musical."

Manchester Guardian.—"Will be welcome to every lover of poetry who takes it up."

21 BEDFORD STREET, LONDON, W.C.

10,000/29/5/91.

www.ingramcontent.com/pod-product-compliance
Lightning Source LLC
Chambersburg PA
CBHW031345070726
47496CB00017B/1728